Puffin Books

Editor: Kaye Webb

THE SPRING ON THE MOUNTAIN

Peter, Michael and Emma weren't at all happy to
find themselves farmed out to Mr and Mrs Myer
for a week's holiday in the country. They were
strangers to each other, the Myers themselves were
strangers to the neighbourhood, and at first the
atmosphere was uncomfortable. Then the children
found themselves with a lot of unanswered
questions.

How was it, for instance, that when Peter looked
into the fisherman's glass float the face he saw
was not his own? Who was the tramp who warned
them not to play at séances, and why did he look
so like the man in the picture on the landing?
Were the starlings really watching them? And were
they right to trust the mysterious Mrs White when
she sent them on a quest up the mountain, along
the ancient Arthur's Way, to find a magical spring,
especially since there was a legend that no one
could spend a night on the mountain and survive?

This is Judy Allen's first novel, and it is an
irresistible combination of everyday life and
powerful fantasy. Sensible, sensitive Emma,
sceptical Michael and imaginative, visionary Peter
are totally believable characters, and doubting,
fearing and wondering with them, we are drawn
into their spell-binding adventure.

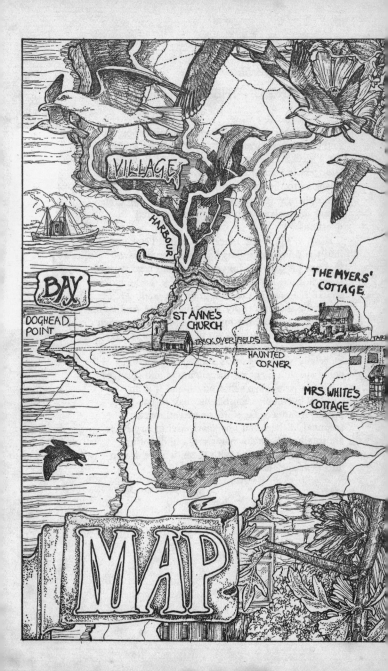

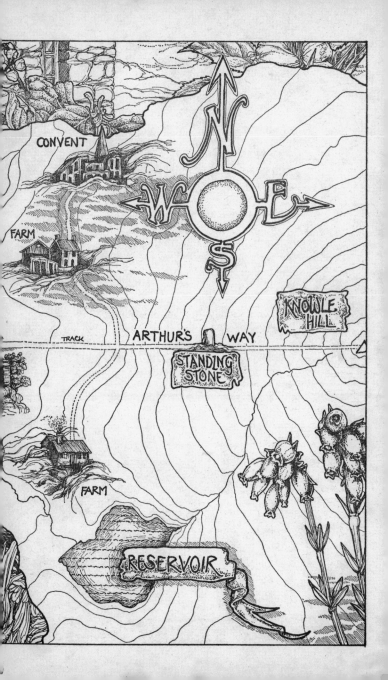

CONVENT

FARM

KNOWLE HILL

TRACK   ARTHUR'S   WAY

STANDING
STONE

FARM

RESERVOIR

Judy Allen

The Spring
on the Mountain

Illustrated by John Hurford

Puffin Books

Puffin Books,
Penguin Books Ltd,
Harmondsworth, Middlesex, England
Penguin Books,
625 Madison Avenue, New York, New York 10022, U.S.A.
Penguin Books Australia Ltd,
Ringwood, Victoria, Australia
Penguin Books Canada Ltd,
2801 John Street, Markham, Ontario, Canada L3R 1B4
Penguin Books (N.Z.) Ltd,
182–190 Wairau Road, Auckland 10, New Zealand

First published by Jonathan Cape Ltd 1973
Published in Puffin Books 1977

Made and printed in Great Britain by
Richard Clay (The Chaucer Press) Ltd,
Bungay, Suffolk
Set in Linotype Pilgrim

To J.M.A.

MRS MYER returned almost at once to the kitchen where her husband was slowly and methodically scraping the mud off his boots on to a sheet of newspaper.

'I have never,' said Mrs Myer, 'known you to be so particular about mud.' She sat down in the chair opposite him as if she was exhausted.

Mr Myer stopped scraping. 'What? Have you given up?'

'It's your turn. I'm not getting anywhere. I've never been so tired. I'd rather plough a field before breakfast than try and drag a word out of those three.'

'I wouldn't be much use,' said Mr Myer complacently, resuming his scraping. 'I'm just a gruff old countryman. What could I say to three little tongue-tied townies?'

Mr Myer had recently retired from his city job to live on

the interest from his savings in a large cottage in a high moorland valley. There was an excellent view, in good weather, of the mountain that rose to the east and, from the top windows or from any patch of high land in the valley, a picturesque seascape to the west. Enough to warm the heart of anyone wanting to get back to nature. To fill their more practical needs the Myers had a large vegetable garden, which would probably produce better results when they understood it more fully.

'You could tell them the old woman wants to meet them,' offered Mr Myer.

'I don't want to deliver them up to her yet. Let's at least try and entertain them ourselves for the first evening.'

There was a knock on the kitchen door and the girl, Emma, came in, carrying the teapot. 'Could I put some more hot water in it?' she said politely.

'Of course,' said Mrs Myer, leaping up and relighting the gas under the kettle. 'You go back to the others and I'll bring it to you.'

Emma hesitated. 'I'm sorry if we're a bit difficult,' she said.

'Not at all,' said Mrs Myer. She liked Emma the best. Michael looked aloof and bored and Peter appeared to be present in body only. But Emma, with her round pink face and shining mousy hair, looked healthy and solid and friendly. And besides, she reminded Mrs Myer of her mother.

'It's a very nice place,' Emma went on helpfully. 'It's just that we've got to make friends with each other.'

Mrs Myer allowed herself to be comforted. 'I expect you're all just tired after your journeys,' she said.

'Yes, that'll be it,' said Emma. 'We'll get used to each other. And it's only for a week, after all.'

Mrs Myer felt a wave of affection for Emma and her

determination. 'It's partly our fault,' she said. 'We just took the first three who answered the advertisement. We didn't try to match up your interests or anything. And in a week you'll be gone and we'll have three more and it was silly of me to think that the first day or so would be anything but – difficult.'

'People are coming right on into the winter, then?' said Emma, obviously reluctant to return to the silent sitting-room.

'Well, we're leaving the advertisement in the magazine. If people want to send children in the winter, that's up to them. It needn't always be for holidays, you see, like you three; sometimes it might be for convalescence. The air here is very good.'

The teapot was refilled and Mrs Myer shepherded Emma back into the front room. Michael was sitting at the tea table, gazing morosely into his empty cup. Peter had quite obviously been inspecting the room and had got as far as the mantelpiece where one or two rather unusual ornaments flanked a small, square-faced, modern clock. For a moment, as Mrs Myer came in at the door, he looked as if he was going to pretend he had just been warming his hands at the fire, but she smiled at him and he relaxed slightly.

'What's this?' he said.

On the corner of the mantelpiece stood a glass globe, the size of a grapefruit, mounted on a dark piece of stone.

'A fisherman's float,' said Mrs Myer. 'For the nets.'

'It looks like a crystal ball.'

'I suppose it does. No, it's just a fisherman's float. You sometimes find them down on the beach. That's probably some sort of local rock it's stuck to, but I don't really know.'

'Did you find it?' said Peter.

'No, it came with the cottage. We rent it partly furnished and quite a lot of the ornaments and pictures came with it.'

'Isn't that annoying?' said Emma. 'Other people's things?'

'They fit in quite well. We didn't bring much with us from London – it wasn't suitable.'

Mrs Myer filled the teacups, and Peter came back to the table and sat down. All three children refused a second piece of cake and silence fell once more. Mrs Myer, who had pictured herself cooking vast meals for eternally hungry and lively twelve-year-olds, sighed and accepted the responsibility of filling the silence. She decided not to fire any more questions at them about their best subjects at school and their hobbies – so that they had to defend their privacy all the time – but to tell them things. So she told them about her problems; about the reason she had put the advertisement in the magazine, which was largely financial but partly because she was lonely; and about the pleasure she had felt when three families had decided to board their children out so near the end of the holidays. She told them about how Mr Myer so enjoyed pottering in the garden that he refused to make any decisions at all, about anything, other than when to plant sprouts – and it had to be admitted that he was usually wrong about that; and about the strange feeling she had that the villagers were going to watch the pair of them very closely for at least two years before they decided whether or not to put warmth into their 'Good mornings'.

The September dusk began to seep out of shadowy corners in the garden and Peter, suddenly animated, asked if they could take a walk before it got too dark. Mrs Myer saw them to the front door and left them to it.

They didn't go far because dusk was short. They simply walked for a few hundred yards in each direction. Turning right out of the gate, they followed the lane between high hedges to the bend, past which it went down to the village itself. When they turned to face the opposite direction they saw that the lane seemed to point right at the mountain, although it disappeared every now and then as the moor undulated. There were two or three cottages not far beyond the Myers', but the rest of the valley, in the direction of the mountain, looked strangely empty to their town-bred eyes.

They walked as far as the farthest cottages. Michael looked at the windows as they passed, expecting to see the curtains twitching back into place, but there was no sign of curiosity at all. By now the mountain was looming very dimly.

'I like that mountain,' said Peter. 'Do you suppose it's possible to go up it?'

'I'm sure it's *possible*,' said Michael.

'I mean would it be possible for us? Right to the top?'

'Well, which is the top?' said Michael. It was a rambling mountain with several high points and it looked as if it probably spread east a very long way.

'That is,' said Peter, as if it was perfectly obvious, and he pointed at a peak that was perhaps marginally higher than the rest.

'How can you be sure?' said Michael, amused.

'I just am. And anyway, look on along this lane to the foot. It seems to point exactly to that peak.'

Emma shivered. 'I don't much like this inky black lane,' she said. 'Shall we go indoors again?'

They passed the cottages once more, and this time they were watched. In the window of the end one stood a tall figure. The cottage was set well back from the lane and the light from the room was behind the figure, so that it was not even possible for Michael to make out if it was a man or a woman. It made no attempt to move out of sight when he looked at it. Michael considered waving, lacked the courage and ignored it.

'We don't all have to go up the mountain just because

Peter wants to,' he said, as they left the watching figure behind them.

Emma glanced over her shoulder at the dark bulk behind which stars were just beginning to appear. 'I wouldn't mind going up it on a nice day, if there was no fog and no danger. There's probably a path. It doesn't look *very* high.'

'Oh it's –' said Peter, and then stopped.

'It's what?' said Michael at last.

Peter blushed. 'I'm just glad it's there,' he said.

In the Myers' sitting-room the table was cleared and there was an open fire burning in the hearth instead of the electric one which had been there when they had arrived. 'I'm trying to do it all *right*,' said Mrs Myer, beaming. She looked anxiously at Emma. 'Do you think I ought to make chutney and jam and things like that?'

'If you want to,' said Emma.

'Well, it's all part of it, isn't it?' said Mrs Myer. 'Unfortunately, one has such a clear idea of what one ought to do in the country. And it all involves very hard work, don't you think?'

'I wouldn't try,' said Michael. 'You should employ rustic servants to do all these rustic things for you.'

'My husband is fussing about in the greenhouse by candle-light,' said Mrs Myer. 'If one of you would like to go and fetch him we can all have a game of cards or something.'

Michael got up.

'Go into the back garden,' Mrs Myer told him, 'and you'll find him surrounded by moths right down at the far end.'

'Is it possible to go up the mountain?' said Emma, as Michael went out.

'I think so,' said Mrs Myer.

'I mean, is it easy?'

'The summer visitors seemed to go up it in ordinary

14

shoes,' said Mrs Myer. 'And as far as I know they all came back. We'd have heard if one of them hadn't, I'm sure.'

'Are there legends?' said Peter.

'Oh yes. I haven't really taken them in properly, though. I'm afraid I've been too busy currying favour with the natives and trying to find out if I'm expected to know how to make herb tea and all that sort of thing. That lane outside is supposed to be haunted, I do know that, down at the bend.'

'But we've just been down there,' said Emma.

'Oh yes, dear, but it's just one of those things. People get ideas. You know how it is. You never see anything yourself, and you never meet anybody who's actually seen anything, either, though you'll quite likely meet someone who's cousin's first wife's brother's best friend saw something.'

'Even so,' said Emma, 'I don't think I'd have gone there in the dusk if I'd known.'

'And there's an old convent at one end of the valley,' went on Mrs Myer, 'with a few strange stories attached to it, I gather. I think they all stem from the Dissolution of the Monasteries, or something, though it's full of very respectable-looking nuns now. And there's an old woman up the lane who I imagine in the Middle Ages would have been the local witch. As a matter of fact, she's our landlord. We rent this cottage from her.'

'Nice!' said Emma.

'Oh, not "witch" in any evil sense. Sort of "Old wise woman", who would know which herb was the right antidote for which snake-bite. That sort of thing. *She's* probably the person to ask if you're interested in local legends. As soon as she heard we had young people coming to stay she said she'd like to meet you. And as it's the first sign of friendship I've managed to get out of her, I confess I promised I'd send you over some time.'

Michael and Mr Myer came into the room.

'So we're all going to play cards,' said Mr Myer, beaming in an avuncular fashion.

'What about the mountain?' said Peter.

'The mountain?' said Mr Myer, thinking Peter was addressing him. 'Ah, well, I don't like it.'

'But it's the main geographical feature around here,' said Michael indignantly, as if that proved something.

'Quite, quite,' said Mr Myer.

'You mean you think it's sinister?' suggested Emma.

'No, no, no. It's probably just that everyone is always talking *about* the mountain, directing one to other villages *by* the mountain, and discussing the weather *on* the mountain. Perhaps I've just got sick of it.' He laughed. 'Where are the cards?'

Mrs Myer went to the desk to get them.

'Is there a legend about the mountain?' Peter persisted.

'Of course,' said Mr Myer, accepting the pack and shuffling it confidently. 'There's a legend about every blade of grass in a place like this. Though I admit I don't know the story properly. It's supposed to be connected with the Holy Grail in some way. And there's an idea that anyone who spends a night up there goes mad or dies. Of course, a night on any mountain wouldn't do you much good.'

Mrs Myer suggested Canasta. None of the children had ever played it before.

'We'll teach you,' said Mr Myer. 'You'll enjoy it.' He launched into a quick run-down of the rules, which confused them all.

'Not to worry,' he said at last. 'Pick it up as we go along. Much the best way.'

Peter got up from the table. 'I'd rather just watch,' he said.

'You come and sit beside me. I'll see that you win,' said Mr Myer.

'No, thank you. I'd rather watch.'

'Someone's got to lose,' said Michael, smiling but not quite enough.

'I'm just not interested in cards,' said Peter, moving over to the fireplace and inspecting the burning logs.

'There are lots of books on those shelves over there,' said Mrs Myer. 'Local guidebooks and things which might interest you.'

'I've got an Uncle,' said Emma, 'who doesn't like cards at all, but he never minds if other people get on and play if they want to. In fact he'd *rather* they did.'

Peter stood and watched the logs burn, and heard, with half his mind, the game get haltingly under way, encouraged loudly by Mr Myer.

He reached up and, very carefully, lifted down the glass ball. Now that he had been told, he could see that it was in fact a fisherman's float. It was hollow – not solid as a crystal would be – and the glass was poor quality and flawed. All the weight seemed to be in the stone it was mounted on, which looked almost like quartz, only much darker in colour, and was rough and unpolished. It was more or less a cube but didn't look as if it had been shaped with much care, if at all. It was rather pleasant to hold, it fitted well into Peter's hands. He looked down into the glass and saw the fire's flames flickering. They began to hurt his eyes and he sat down on a low stool, with his back to the side of the mantelpiece and the ornament in his lap. Now he could see his own face, poorly reflected and convex. Just as he had let his hearing become blurred, so that the Canasta game was reduced to a murmur, he now let his eyes drift out of focus, too. This was something he often did if he felt out of place in his surroundings.

Suddenly he realized that the face in the glass ball was no longer misty but very clear. There was a dark circle and a face, and it wasn't his face at all, it was an old woman's face. He was looking down into a well and reflected in the water at the bottom was the face of an old woman with the moonlit sky behind her and the branch of a tree curving over her head. Then he realized that in fact it was he who was at the bottom of the well, looking up its dark shaft, and the old woman was at the top, bending over the rim and looking down at him. This sudden reversal of the picture made him dizzy and he looked up from the globe to give his eyes a chance to adjust. When he looked back he saw, once more, his own face, poorly reflected and convex.

He got up and put the float back where he had found it. His consciousness was once more filled with the seemingly interminable game of Canasta, which had in fact only been going on for ten minutes. He looked at the four intent faces and decided he was not in the right company to talk about what had happened. He fetched a book, which made Mrs Myer smile, and sat with it open on his lap so that no one would interrupt him while he tried to think.

2 THE next day there was fog. Not unusual for September, but it upset everybody rather, particularly Mrs Myer who was afraid her guests would be bored. Michael, in fact, was, and he persuaded the others that they should go for a walk regardless. 'Not on to the moor in fog,' said Mrs Myer. 'You'll think I'm just being fussy, but you *will* get lost and you'll sink into a quagmire and what will I tell your parents?' Emma told her not to worry. 'Well keep to the lane,' she said. 'We'll probably go down to the village.'

Muffled up against the white vapour, they left Mr Myer happily cataloguing his gardening catalogues and Mrs Myer baking what she called a Country Pie, which to most people would have looked rather like a steak-and-kidney pie.

They wandered along the lane, not speaking, and at the

corner – the haunted corner – they stopped, all of them at once, as if they had agreed to. The leaves of the high hedges were wet and nothing else was visible – just the hedges and a short stretch of lane behind and before them. Michael kicked a stone which made a muted, muffled sound, as if it had been made soggy by the clinging dampness.

'This is silly,' said Emma, after a couple of minutes. 'Not in broad daylight, surely.'

'Not very broad,' said Michael. 'Rather narrow, I should have thought.'

'But surely only at night?' said Emma. 'Can't we go on? It isn't warm enough to stand about like this.'

'What's it haunted by?' said Michael to Peter.

'*I* don't know.'

'I thought you were reading some folklore book or other last night – while we played cards.'

'I didn't see any mention of this lane.'

'What were you reading about, then? Your lovely mountain?'

'I didn't take in what I was reading,' said Peter. 'Your noisy card game was a bit distracting.'

'You should have played too,' said Michael. 'It looked extremely rude.'

'Oh, but people don't expect you to play cards if you don't want to,' said Emma quickly.

'I happen to find card games a silly waste of time, that's all,' said Peter.

'Well, which particular intellectual pursuit would you have preferred? I didn't hear you making any suggestions.'

'I don't care how other people waste their time, so long as they don't drag me into it.'

'I can assure you nobody wanted to drag you into it. It went much better without you. But what's all this about "waste of time"? What are we all supposed to be doing all the time? Did we offend you by enjoying ourselves without you, or what?'

'You weren't enjoying yourselves. You looked thoroughly embarrassed by the whole stupid thing and Emma looked as if she thought she'd be shot if she didn't understand all the rules. All that effort – for nothing!'

'I'm sure that your blunt Yorkshire manner is supposed to be endearing and refreshing,' said Michael, 'but in fact you strike me as supercilious and rude. The Myers were entertaining us. Therefore one should go along with things unless one has something better that one can suggest without offending anybody.'

'That's a silly social convention,' said Peter. 'I didn't want to play and there was no reason why I should. You said yourself it was better without me.'

'Whatwasthat?' said Emma, all in one word.

Michael ignored her but Peter, who could hear a strange wheezing that seemed to be approaching from the direction of the village, turned to her and said, 'What?'

'Something brushed past my legs,' said Emma, 'but I didn't see what it was. It was wet.'

The wheezing became an angry snorting and something white burst out of the barrier of mist and headed straight for them. Emma, who was in its path, jumped back, and the bull-terrier with the pig-like face scurried on up the lane.

'That was a dog,' said Michael patiently. 'And it is chasing a cat. And the cat is wet because so is everything in this fog.'

Emma, to hide that she had been really frightened, set off at speed, crying, 'We must save the cat.'

'All right, so we go in the other direction,' said Michael with resignation, and they followed the already blurry figure of Emma up the lane, past the Myers' house and as far as the end cottage on the right, now quite invisible from the lane.

By the time they caught up with the dog it was trying to cram its broad shoulders through a gap in the fence, snarling horribly. The source of its rage had stopped running, once its slimmer form had negotiated the gap, and was just visible sitting in the middle of the path, washing its black face with one black paw. Emma out of genuine concern, and Michael out of politeness to her, made ineffectual shooing gestures at the bull-terrier's feverishly wriggling hind-quarters.

'Just wait,' said a voice. 'The storm will abate in a few seconds.'

Peter looked up first and caught a glimpse, as the fog shifted slightly, of a very tall figure in the cottage garden, magnified by the mist, who surveyed them owlishly through an enormous pair of spectacles. The picture faded and then out of the fog, much nearer at hand, stepped the smaller, though still tall, figure of an old woman. She had taken off the large glasses that had given her her owlish aspect. Emma and Michael straightened up to face her and the dog extricated itself from the fence and waddled away down the lane, coughing.

The old woman leant on the fence and smiled. 'There was no need for you to bother,' she said. 'Though it was kind of you. The dog has lived at that end of the lane as long as the cat has lived at this. There is a permanent state of conflict but never a confrontation. The one you should be sorry for is the bull-terrier. He has very little control over his emotions and is constantly taunted and frustrated by this animal, who should know better.'

There was a slight pause and then Emma said, 'Oh – well, I'm glad the cat's all right.'

'What very unpleasant weather you've brought with you,'

said the old woman. 'Never mind. Tomorrow will be fine. Would you like to come in out of the fog and have a hot cup of something?'

Emma automatically looked at Michael.

Michael said, 'That's very kind of you but we were just going to walk to the village.'

Peter said nothing. He was far too amazed to find himself looking at the face that he had seen in the glass ball the night before.

'You are rather a formal young man,' said the old woman, 'so I will introduce myself properly. I am the Myers' landlord. I don't know if they have any irreverent nicknames for me, but you may call me Mrs White. A walk to the village would be extremely damp and unpleasant this morning. Cocoa or coffee in front of a log fire would be far more suitable. This way.'

She turned from the fence and proceeded slowly up the path towards the cottage. Michael shrugged, and held the gate open for the other two.

'Mrs Myer's old witch-woman,' Emma whispered, as she went into the garden past him.

'Oh well,' said Michael lightly, 'so long as we're not ingredients in some recipe of hers.'

Peter brushed past the other two on the long path as if he was going to catch up with Mrs White and then, jerkily, stopped and hung back until they caught up with him. 'What's the matter with you?' said Michael, but Peter drew away from them again and this time he did catch up with Mrs White, just as she reached her front door.

His words reached the other two quite clearly. 'Have you got a well?'

Mrs White turned round to look at him and smiled. 'Yes, of course,' she said. 'It's in the back garden. Shall we go and look at it?' And she turned away from the front door and led them round the little house by a gravel path.

Emma and Michael looked at each other, mystified, and then followed the two figures ahead of them. As they crossed some damp grass, the well loomed out of the fog. Peter put his hands on the rim and leant forward to look down it, but it was full of fog and he couldn't see the water. He looked up and a branch of an apple tree curved over his head. He looked down along the branch to the trunk. It was an old tree and it leant towards the well, almost as if trying to dip the branch into it. Mrs White watched with friendly interest but no surprise.

'Have you got a particular interest in wells?' said Michael at last.

'Let's go in out of the fog,' said Mrs White, and she ushered Peter ahead of her along the path to the open front door. Michael and Emma trailed along behind them. In the hall Peter turned to Mrs White, blocking the doorway, his fog-damp hair plastered to his head, and said, 'Where did you find the glass ball?'

Mrs White raised her eyebrows slightly and smiled. 'Why, on the beach,' she said. 'It's just a fisherman's float.' She waited, but Peter seemed to be at a loss.

'Come along,' she said, and at last they all managed to get into the warm sitting-room, which was as stuffed with things as old ladies' rooms often are. There were books, some of them very old, and plants, some of them most unusual, and things everywhere, on every flat surface: things they wanted to pick up, and look at, or just touch; stones and shells and little carvings, tiny boxes, silver bottles, delicate oriental figures and aggressive African wood-carvings. On the wall opposite the fireplace was an enormous astrological chart, and over the mantelpiece hung three oval silver frames, linked together to form a triptych. In the first was a painting of the head and shoulders of a

24

young girl, very beautiful, but with strength in her face –
no simpering Victorian maiden. In the central frame was the
portrait of a woman, equally beautiful, older and with a
greater dignity. The third frame held a mirror. The triptych
caught Emma's eye immediately, and then, as she looked,
Mrs White moved across behind her so that her face was
reflected in the mirror. It was immediately apparent that
the first two pictures were portraits of herself. 'If one thinks,
perhaps, that one doesn't wish to be old,' she said, 'it is good
to be reminded that one is merely completing something
designed a very long time ago.'

This embarrassed Emma. She searched for something to
say, could only connect the old woman in her mind with
legends and odd happenings, and said, 'The lane is
haunted.'

She said it as a statement, although she meant it to be a
question, and Mrs White said, 'Do you know that, or have
you just been told? Come and sit close to the fire, you're
all very damp.'

They avoided the fireside wing chair that was so obviously hers, and Emma and Michael sat on the sofa directly
in front of the fire and Peter on a stool on the other side of it.

'Mrs Myer mentioned it,' said Emma. 'Is it true?'

'Oh yes, it's true,' said Mrs White.

'But have *you* ever seen anything there?' said Michael,
whose confidence was returning with the fire's warmth.

'Many things,' said Mrs White, serious-faced and heavy-
lidded. 'Leaves on hedges, birds on twigs, people passing
to and fro with their shopping ...'

Michael forced a pinched smile at what he thought was a
very weak joke. 'I wondered if you'd seen a ghost,' he said.

'I haven't seen anything out of the ordinary,' said Mrs
White. 'Now, what would you all like to drink? Coffee?
You're sure? Very well, I won't be long.'

'But what's the lane haunted *by*?' said Emma, desperate for one answer that wouldn't beg another question.

'It's haunted by cold fear,' said Mrs White simply, and went out of the room and closed the door quietly behind her.

Michael flung himself back against the cushions of the sofa. 'Oh boy!' he said.

'What?' said Emma.

'She's a crazy old woman with an over-developed sense of the dramatic. What an exit line!' He mimicked in a falsetto, quite unlike the old woman's deep and serious voice, 'It's haunted by cold fear, actually, nothing more, I'll just get the coffee.'

Emma turned to Peter. 'Why did you suddenly ask if she had a well?'

Peter shifted slightly. He had just realized he was sitting in the same position in this room as he had occupied in the Myers' room when he had looked into the float. He had the feeling that everything that was happening now had happened already, and although he knew that this was only because he was in the same position, he felt as if he knew what Michael was going to say.

'Yes, what about that?' said Michael, and they both stared at him, and Peter found he had forgotten what he had thought Michael was going to say.

He told them exactly why he had asked.

When he had finished they both continued to stare at him for a moment and then Michael said, 'Oh, rubbish.'

'Don't be so crushing,' said Emma.

'Why didn't you tell her, what's-her-name, Mrs White?' asked Michael.

'There was no point, it was so obvious that she knew.'

'She knew you knew and you knew she knew you knew she knew, you mean?'

'Yes.'

'But how could it happen?' said Emma, glancing over her shoulder at the door.

'It couldn't,' said Michael. 'It was an optical illusion. He was seeing his own face, but he'd stared at the fire and his eyes couldn't see straight.'

'I recognized her as soon as I saw her over the fence,' said Peter.

'There's probably a picture of her in the Myers' cottage, along with all her other stuff. You'd probably seen it before and you looked in the float and then imagined that you saw it *in* the float.'

'I haven't seen any picture of her.'

'Unconsciously.'

'There isn't a picture of her at the Myers'.'

'I bet you there is. Probably on the landing or somewhere like that, where one sees things without really taking them in.'

'I tell you there is no picture of her there.'

'We'll look thoroughly when we get back. I'd bet money on it.'

'And don't say anything to her about it,' said Peter.

'All right,' said Michael magnanimously.

'Not because it didn't happen,' said Peter sharply. 'I just don't want her to think I've been gossiping about it.'

'Of course, of course,' said Michael, deliberately oozing disbelief.

'Would you please open the door?' came Mrs White's voice from the other side of it. Michael hurried to do this and to take the tray from her. She signed to him to put it on the floor in front of the fire and then, sitting in her chair and bending forward rather stiffly, she handed round the mugs of coffee.

'Is that all the legends say?' said Michael, as if there had

27

been no break in the conversation at all. 'That the lane is haunted by cold fear?'

'Not at all,' said Mrs White. 'The corner is quite heavily populated with ghosts. A headless horseman, of course. A white lady, naturally. And I believe there's a hanged man, too, with the noose still around his neck. They've all got stories, but the stories evolved to explain the apparitions so they are not necessarily historically true. The gallows, for instance, was never at that spot but a good four miles away.'

'But are the ghosts real?' said Emma, and Michael laughed, not unkindly.

'At some time,' said Mrs White, 'fear has been felt at that place, very, very strongly. No one knows what the cause of the fear was, and it doesn't really matter. That's gone long ago. But the emotion itself has become trapped and repeats itself in an endless cycle. The mind usually has to make reasons for such a sensation, and people tend to see whatever they expect or whatever they fear most when it comes upon them. There's no danger, but don't wait about there. If it does come, it isn't nice.'

Michael said, 'But fear is something you feel inside you, it isn't something that comes out of you and hangs about in the air.'

'You're so sure?'

'If something nasty happened to you at a particular place,' said Michael, 'and you were frightened, and then you passed the place again, even a long time later, I can see that you'd probably feel fear again. It would be memory, that's all. But no one else passing that place would feel anything.'

'Then why do they?'

'Because they've heard the corner is haunted.'

'And how has the story evolved? And why does a cat which has never been to a vet before show fear the moment it is carried inside the door and exposed to the lingering fear of thousands of other animals?'

'I just find it very difficult to believe that a chunk of "emotion" is floating about in the air in the lane,' said Michael uncomfortably.

'What sort of things do you find it easy to believe, Michael?'

'I believe what my eyes tell me,' said Michael.

'Oh dear,' said Mrs White, throwing up her hands in a parody of horror. 'You really believe all *that* illusion? Oh, this is terrible!'

Michael was beginning to redden. He had thought he was in command of the conversation. Now he was not so sure.

'Do you really believe that the mug in my hand is smaller than the mug in your hand, because that's what your eyes tell you,' went on Mrs White. 'Haven't they taught you to draw at school? Haven't you learnt about perspective? Do you believe that a long straight road really runs to a point at the far end? Or that the poplars on the other side of a river are truly half the height of the ones on this side? The lenses of our eyes are curved, Michael. We don't see reality.'

'Yes, all right, I know,' said Michael, looking deflated but unrepentant.

Mrs White, who had been leaning forward in her chair and examining him with some intensity, relaxed and smiled. 'It's important not to brush aside what one doesn't understand,' she said gently. 'For instance, there is this stone that I don't understand but I know that it "works", if that's the right word.' From underneath a pot-stand beside her chair, she lifted a large and heavy chunk of rock, which they had not noticed before. She lifted it into her lap.

Peter sat forward sharply and almost tipped himself off his stool. 'The float is stuck to a piece like that,' he said.

'*That's* it,' said Mrs White, almost as if she had waited a long time for him to notice. She held the stone in her hands, warming it, and she looked down at it with a soft dreamy expression on her face. She had her back to the window and the fog made the room dim. The left side of her thin but strongly boned face was outlined by the firelight and the right side was shadowy. When she looked down at the stone her eyes were filled with shadow, which gave her an oddly mask-like appearance.

Peter watched her carefully. Michael's discomfiture seemed to grow. Emma held her own hand, very tightly, in her lap, and wished to go home.

Mrs White began to speak, very softly and very slowly. 'Somewhere – it is dark. There is a dark place and it is cold. Cold and dark. And something is moving in the cold dark.'

While she spoke there seemed to be a great stillness in the room, and Emma thought that her heart had stopped and that if the cold and the dark and the something that moved there seeped out of the stone towards her, she would die.

But Mrs White stopped, and smiled, and replaced the stone gently, and spread her hands and said, 'You see? But I can't interpret. What the stone tells is true, I know, but I don't know if it foretells the future, or retells the past, or even speaks of the present. It may be that at this moment, in the cold vault of some ruined Mayan temple, a snake uncoils from sleep. It's quite possible. Or it may be that the stone remembers where it came from when' – She paused, glanced at Peter, then lowered her eyes and went on – 'when miners moved through the cold dark to steal it from its place. One day I hope I will understand, but I never will if I dismiss the whole thing as nonsense. I've enjoyed your visit so much, you will all come and see me again, won't you?'

This last sentence followed on so smoothly from the rest of her speech that it was a moment before they realized that they had all finished their coffee and had been gently dismissed.

'Yes. Thank you,' said Emma, jumping up.

Mrs White saw them to the door. 'I can't wave good-bye,' she said mildly, 'because you'll be swallowed up by the fog within six yards of me.'

'Thank you very much,' said Peter at the door.

'Thank you for the coffee,' said Emma.

'Yes, thanks,' said Michael, and led the way rapidly down the path. The door clicked shut behind them.

'Nutty as a fruit cake,' said Michael.

'It's nice,' said Peter angrily, 'to know that I'm not the only one who's supercilious and rude. They say you see your own faults in other people.'

3 PETER set off down the lane towards the Myers' house at a tremendous pace, leaving Michael behind. Emma wasn't sure whether to hurry on with him or hang back with Michael. She adjusted her pace so that the three of them walked strung out in a long line, but Michael caught up with her.

'I don't know how you put up with him,' he began at once.

'Who?' said Emma, hoping to think of a way of avoiding the conversation.

'He lives in the clouds,' said Michael. 'Just because he *thought* it was a crystal ball when he first saw it ...'

'Just because he's interested in things you don't happen to be interested in ...'

'Did you swallow that about the stone?' said Michael.

'Yes, I did,' said Emma, 'and don't talk about the lane any more. I don't like to think about it.'

Peter had left the front door open for them and coils of fog had preceded them into the hall. Michael walked straight up the stairs and disappeared from view.

The hall smelt of fog, steak-and-kidney pie, cabbage and floor polish. Emma shut the front door and watched the streaks of fog as they wound themselves round the banisters and the hatstand and gradually dispersed. All the doors from the hall were shut. The grandfather clock indicated that it was twenty past twelve. The sound of saucepans being moved about on the stove came from the kitchen. Emma hoped that lunch wasn't until at least one o'clock because she didn't feel hungry. She stood and looked at herself in the long mirror opposite the sitting-room door. Her hair was wet and straight and her face, in the dark hall, white.

'Are you coming in?' said Peter, and she saw him reflected over her shoulder in the sitting-room doorway. She hung her coat on the hallstand and went into the sitting-room where the large table was laid for lunch.

'Do we have to do things together just because we're staying here together?' said Peter.

Not doing things together hadn't occurred to Emma.

'We didn't choose each other,' said Peter. 'I don't see why we have to feel tied together. You're all right, but Michael spoils everything.'

'Oh no,' said Emma. 'I'm sure he doesn't mean to.'

'He was so rude,' said Peter, in a more subdued voice. 'I'm sure he doesn't think he was. He opens doors and carries trays and then makes it quite clear to her that he thinks she's mad, or stupid or something.'

'She wasn't offended,' said Emma.

'Hardly. She wouldn't care what some silly kid thought of her.'

'It sounds funny to hear you say that. I always think of Michael as older than you.'

'He's always *dressed* so tidily.'

'He can dress how he likes,' said Emma sharply.

The sitting-room door opened and let in the sound of the clock striking half past twelve and Mrs Myer carrying a pile of hot dinner-plates which she put down on the table.

'I quite forgot to tell you when to get back for lunch,' she said. 'And here you are at just the right time. I should have known your stomachs would lead you.'

Mr Myer came in behind her carrying a pie that would have served twelve. Mrs Myer hurried out again. Peter went to the door and called Michael. Emma watched with a sinking heart as a dish of potatoes, a dish of carrots in a thick white sauce and a dish of cabbage appeared on the table, one after the other.

Michael came in and they sat round in silence and watched as Mrs Myer piled their plates nauseatingly high with food. No one spoke much during the actual meal. The three children concentrated on trying to push down as much food as possible and were conscious of the expression of disappointment on Mrs Myer's face as each at last admitted defeat.

'It's just that we didn't have a proper walk this morning,' said Emma, averting her eyes from the quantities of food that still remained in front of her. 'I have an Uncle who always loses his appetite when there's a fog.'

'The fog is clearing slightly,' said Mrs Myer, collecting up the plates. 'Fancy Mrs White making sure she met you so soon,' she went on, brightening up. 'She must have been watching for you.'

'She watched us when we went up the lane yesterday evening,' said Michael. 'Not that I knew it was her then.'

They helped to carry the dishes out and Emma noticed

with dismay a large bowl, on the kitchen table, above whose rim golden-brown-and-white peaks of meringue were visible.

'Don't forget,' said Mrs Myer, as she served them to large platefuls of pudding, 'to tell me if Mrs White let drop any hints.'

'Like what?' said Michael.

'Well – like, "This is the season of the year for digging in loam," or something like that. You can laugh, Michael, but that's how one learns to fit in in the country, you know – by picking up stray remarks.'

'I think you only hear that kind of stray remark on the radio,' said Michael.

Because the Myers did not normally talk much during meals – although Mr Myer made one or two remarks about town-dwellers' appetites and how the country air was sure to improve them – it was not until everything was being carried out to the kitchen that Mrs Myer began to make conversation in earnest, asking about their visit. Mr Myer insisted on doing the washing-up, and when the others returned to the fire Michael launched into a description of Mrs White and her stone.

Mrs Myer listened with eyes that grew wider and a mouth that trembled more and more obviously. As the story ended, she began to giggle. 'I don't *believe* it,' she said. 'She's never talked like that to me. I wonder if she saves it for what she takes to be gullible children. *That's* why she was so keen to meet you all.'

Michael was disconcerted. He had expected Mrs Myer to be interested but now, although she more or less reflected his own earlier attitude, he was unsure what to say.

'I think she's quite sincere,' he said primly.

Mrs Myer reached out to pick up one of the logs waiting by the hearth. Regardless of its rough bark and its surprised population of woodlice, she hugged it to her and declaimed,

'Ah yes, ah yes, I can see the tree it came from, I can see the woodman's axe rising, I can hear the scream of pain as it falls on the trunk ...'

Michael blushed faintly and glanced at Peter. Peter stared straight back at him, icily, and offered no help.

'I've told it wrong,' said Michael, with an effort. 'I'm sure if you'd been there ...' He couldn't have told why he was upset, and to his annoyance and confusion he realized that any words he now used might be Mrs White's – 'Don't laugh at things you don't understand.'

'If I'd been there I wouldn't have known where to look,' interrupted Mrs Myer. 'How did you manage not to giggle? I can just picture you all sitting there, avoiding each other's eyes ...'

'No,' said Michael stiffly, looking again for support from Peter and then realizing that he had to do it by himself. 'It wasn't like that at all. And it was extremely nice of her to tell us so much, she didn't need to.'

'I'm sorry, dear,' said Mrs Myer, subdued at last. 'I didn't mean to offend you.'

'That's quite all right,' said Michael. 'It was my fault for passing the story on.'

This time when he looked at Peter, Peter smiled at him. Michael was torn between relief and irritation. Mrs Myer put the log back in its place and picked a few pieces of bark off her jumper. 'I'm very sorry,' she repeated. 'I hadn't realized you would take that sort of thing seriously.' Then, brightly, 'Let's play cards.'

It was a stiff and uncomfortable game of cards. The children wished Mrs Myer didn't feel she had to entertain them – as if the weather was her fault – and so did she, but no one liked to say so. They were sick of cards, the game held no one's attention and Peter, who tried to play, couldn't follow it. When Mr Myer joined them he fetched a pack of

Lexicon cards, 'for a change', but somehow no one knew how to play Lexicon, not even Mr Myer, and there were no rules in the pack.

'Well then, *I* know what,' said Mrs Myer. 'We'll have a séance.'

Mr Myer rolled up his eyes and winked at Michael, as if to say 'these foolish women'. Emma looked startled.

'Haven't you played that?' said Mrs Myer. 'You put all the letters of the alphabet on a polished table, in a circle, and then you put a tumbler in the centre, upside down. Everybody sits round the table and puts one finger on the edge of the base of the glass, very lightly. Then, if there's a spirit present, it uses the glass to spell out a message.' She giggled, as if she wasn't sure whether or not she believed it herself.

'Load of rubbish,' said Mr Myer, getting a glass out of the wall-cupboard nevertheless.

'Have any of you ever played?' persisted Mrs Myer.

Michael and Emma said they had not, but Peter said, 'It isn't a game.'

'Well, it's fun anyway,' said Mrs Myer, laying the Lexicon cards round the big table. 'Must be careful to put them clockwise,' she said. 'We might get a nasty spirit if we put them anti-clockwise.'

Peter scowled.

Emma said, 'I don't think I really want to do it.'

'It's the perfect afternoon,' said Mrs Myer. 'A nice, creepy fog and dim lighting in here – all children like to be scared sometimes.' She took her place at the table and Mr Myer found himself a pad and took out his pen. 'Have to have someone to write down what it says,' he explained.

'I don't think it's a good idea,' said Peter.

'Oh, come on,' said Michael, who now thought he had to make amends to Mrs Myer. He sat down opposite her and

Emma sat between them with her back to the window, solid and stocky and serious.

'You don't have to join us, Peter,' said Mrs Myer. 'You can read a book again if you like.'

'Do we have to decide which of us is going to push the glass?' said Michael lightly.

'No,' said Mrs Myer. 'Nobody must push it. It really moves, you know. Though I think it would be better if Peter would sit down because then there would be four of us and it would be more balanced.'

Peter sat down. 'I've never taken part before,' he said, 'but I've seen it done. It doesn't always work. And I think we ought to have something serious to ask it if we're going to do it properly.'

'All right,' said Mrs Myer. 'You choose what we're going to ask.'

'I'd like to know about the mountain,' said Peter after a pause.

Mrs Myer stretched out her arm and rested her forefinger on the glass. 'We'll let it warm up before we ask it anything,' she said. The other three each put a finger on the glass and they sat and waited in silence. Emma began a nervous giggle but Peter frowned at her and she stopped. A log fell to pieces in the grate and sparks streamed up the chimney. Mr Myer's watch turned out to have a very loud tick. Michael's stomach rumbled softly and Emma stifled another giggle. And then the glass began to move.

It moved lightly and, just now, very slowly, and it shocked all three children because it was somehow apparent that no one was pushing it, and that if someone had been it would have been possible to tell who it was. It moved in slow circles in the centre of the table and Emma said quietly, 'I think I'd like to stop.' No one responded, and then Peter said, 'Too late.'

At last the glass headed for the outside of the table and began to butt at the letters in turn. Mr Myer wrote M, P, Z, D, H. The glass returned to the centre of the table and resumed its slow circling. 'Rubbish,' said Mr Myer. 'Lost its vowels.'

'It's only checking where the letters are,' said Mrs Myer. 'Keep your hand quite steady, Emma dear, you can change hands if your arm is beginning to ache.'

The glass was on its way again. P, Mr Myer wrote. Then there was a long paused and then M, T followed by M, T again – and more forcefully, so that T was knocked on to the floor and Michael had to pick it up and replace it. D, G, R, spelt the glass deliberately. Mr Myer's loud voice read out what it had said. 'Doesn't make sense so far,' he said, as if he had never expected it to.

All at once the glass began to revolve very quickly in the centre of the table, and then it set off at tremendous speed, tapping at the letters almost too quickly for Mr Myer to write them down. Michael called them out to him. The glass returned to the centre and stood still, as if exhausted. Mr Myer read out what he had. 'Dotry Toread,' said Mr Myer. 'Nonsense again, I'm afraid.'

'Don't you know what it says?' said Peter.

'Dotry Toread,' said Mr Myer.

'Put the spaces differently, 'It's "Do Try To Read".'

'Let's not do it any more,' said Emma.

'We must ask it something,' said Mrs Myer. 'Do you have a message for anyone here?'

The glass stood where it was.

'Do you have a message for me?' said Peter.

The glass revolved two or three times and then glided over to P, where it stopped.

'Is it about the mountain?' said Peter.

M, T, the glass responded.

Emma let out a little sigh and at that moment, foggy though it was, a shadow passed across the window behind her.

'What about the mountain?' said Peter in a soft voice. Emma glanced behind her at the window and even Michael, who was sideways on to it, seemed to notice something.

D, said the glass, slowly and ponderously.

The door into the hall was slightly ajar. A very faint shuffling noise came from the porch.

N, said the glass.

The sound from the porch was slightly louder the second time and Mr Myer raised his head inquiringly from his pad.

G, said the glass.

Mr Myer put down pad, pocketed pen and made for the door.

R, said the glass, and simultaneously there was a heavy thump on the front door. Everybody jumped and the glass fell over on its side and rolled to the edge of the table, where the different texture of the cards was just enough to stop it.

Mr Myer opened the front door and from where they sat they could see, leaning against the porch wall, an old tramp. He was wearing a long, battered, blue reefer coat, tied up with a piece of string which had several newspapers – presumably his bedding – tucked into it. An old fisherman's hat with a pom-pom on it was pulled far down on his head, and his grey hair hung well over his collar. He had a thick, grey, patriarchal beard and very bright eyes.

'Something to eat?' he said.

'Ah! Of course!' said Mr Myer, somewhat taken aback. Mrs Myer bustled out into the kitchen, promising to find something, and the three children got up but stayed well inside the sitting-room where they could see what was going on through the open door.

'I bet she thinks *he* knows a thing or two about country ways,' said Michael.

The old tramp began to point at the sitting-room door. The children drew back still farther, in case they were visible, but he only pointed, he didn't look. 'You don't want to let kids play that game,' he said to Mr Myer. 'That game with the glass.'

Emma clutched Michael's arm. 'How does he *know?*' she whispered.

'Listen,' said Peter.

'Frighten themselves to no good purpose,' said the tramp. 'Grown man like you should know better.'

'We'd better not listen,' whispered Michael. 'He's em-barrassing old Myer. He looked through the window, Emma. Didn't you see him? I thought you had, you looked round.'

'I saw a shadow.'

'You're lucky. I saw a great hairy face, but only for a second. I thought we were conjuring up apparitions, till he knocked at the front door.'

They withdrew to the fireplace.

'He's right, though,' said Peter. 'We shouldn't play games like that.'

Mrs Myer's voice was in the hall now and the tramp was thanking her and saying something about the fog clearing very shortly. Indeed, the room did seem noticeably lighter.

'Let's find something we *want* to do before they come back,' said Emma. 'Or we may have to do this again.' She began to collect up the Lexicon cards.

'How do *you* think it works?' Peter asked Michael curiously.

'I'm still thinking about it,' said Michael. 'By the way, I've been waiting to tell you – I had a good look round before lunch. You're right, there isn't a picture of Mrs White here. But I've just realized there is one of the tramp.'

John Hilford

4 'ARE you serious?' said Peter.

'I'm not sure,' said Michael. 'Come up to the landing and have a look.'

The doors from the first landing opened into the Myers' bedroom, the bathroom and an enormous airing-cupboard. The next flight of stairs led to the attic and the three tiny bedrooms where the children slept in a row, like owls under the rafters. On the wall at the foot of this flight hung four little framed watercolours.

'I must have passed them a dozen times,' said Michael, 'but they're so pale and washy I didn't really notice them until I was looking for pictures.'

The first three paintings were of scenery but the fourth was a portrait. Michael lifted it carefully from its minuscule nail and carried it into the bathroom and over to the window where, as the fog began to lift in earnest, there was more light.

'It should have been done in oils,' he said, which was quite true. The artist had tried to portray a man of about twenty-five, or perhaps thirty, with a tanned face and golden-brown eyes; but the delicate water-colours entirely failed to convey the strength that was obviously meant to show in the square, bearded face.

'I see what you mean,' said Peter after a pause. 'It *could* be him about fifty years ago, but I think it's only because of the beard, really.'

'*This* beard is quite short,' said Michael, 'and brown. *His* beard is grey and twice the length, and yet it still looks like him to me. The eyes, too, and they're an unusual colour.'

'I see what you mean, but the beard is the same shape, basically,' said Peter, 'and I think that's what does it. I mean, it can't really be a picture of him.'

'Why not?' said Emma. 'He's probably about the same age as her.'

'The long lost Mr White, you think?' said Michael.

'I bet you she painted these,' said Emma. 'He may not be long lost – she may know he wanders off every now and then.'

'It would explain the poshy accent,' said Peter, 'but the Myers would know him.'

'They've only been here since spring,' said Emma, reluctant to lose her romantic theory. 'He may have had the urge to wander just before that.'

'I can't really see that rather refined old lady married to him,' said Michael.

'Just because he dresses raggedly –'

'Come on!' said Michael. 'Wanders round for half the year and then begs for food two doors down the lane from her?'

'No, I suppose not.'

A heavy footstep sounded on the stairs behind them. 'Where've you all got to?' said Mr Myer.

Michael carried the picture on to the landing and showed it to him. 'We were just thinking,' he said, 'that this picture looks rather like that old tramp.'

Mr Myer looked at it. 'Does, too,' he said with a laugh. 'Bit younger, though.'

'Well, we wondered if perhaps it *is* a picture of him,' said Michael.

Mr Myer looked blank.

'Painted a long time ago,' explained Emma.

'That'd be a bit of a coincidence,' said Mr Myer. 'See what you mean when you say it's *like* him, but I don't think it *is* him. It's the beard that does it.'

'Yes,' said Peter. 'I think so, too.'

'Oh well, it was an interesting thought,' said Michael. He put the picture back on its nail and peered in the dim light at the other three.

'Are you all coming down, then?' said Mr Myer.

'Do you know who painted these?' said Michael.

'Came with the house, like so many things. You'd have to ask Mrs White.'

'What happened to Mr White?' said Emma.

'Killed in the war. First World War, that is.' He turned down the stairs again and Emma, after glancing over the boys' shoulders at the other three paintings, followed him. The pictures were very dull. There were two views of the mountain: one distant one which, because of faulty technique, made it look like a hill; and one painted as if from the foot, with the mountain filling up the picture and a pattern of stars visible in the dark sky at the top. The third painting was an attempt to represent a mountain stream gushing out over a rock and falling down to the corner of the picture.

44

'Not a great artist, whoever it was,' said Michael. 'Look here, the fog has really lifted and the sun is practically out. For goodness' sake, let's really go for a proper walk. We've been here for twenty-four hours and we haven't been farther than the corner of the lane.'

With something very like relief the two generations parted company.

'If you're not groping through fog you're battling against the wind,' said Michael crossly, dragging the front door shut behind him.

'It was the wind that got rid of the fog,' said Emma, excusing it.

'Fairly obviously, yes,' said Michael waspishly.

The top of the mountain was still invisible, and the leaves that the wind tossed about on the garden path still soggy and limp. Michael opened the front gate and let Emma walk out into the lane ahead of him. She turned to the left to face the moor – so sharply that she walked, quite literally, right into the arms of the tramp, who had been leaning against the fence. She was far too shocked to scream but leapt back from the dirty gaberdine and the damp newspapers and the moist beard, cannoning into Michael, who was just behind her. The tramp just stood there facing them, nodding and smiling, his arms raised slightly as if either to prevent them from passing or to catch the next one who rushed at him. Peter never seemed disposed to start conversations, and as always Emma turned her anxious face to Michael so that he was forced to say, 'What do you want?'

The tramp continued to smile, mostly at Emma, so that at first, forgetting the man's rational conversation with Mr Myer, Michael thought that he was quite mad, and could only hope that it was a gentle kind of madness, because he was much bigger than they had realized, very tall and solidly built.

Then, as though suddenly becoming aware that his stance was threatening, the tramp dropped his arms to his sides and leant back against the fence, making it quite clear that they were free to pass him. 'You gave me a jump,' he said, not sounding at all mad.

This encouraged Michael, who said, with more assurance, 'What are you waiting about here for? You were given food, weren't you?'

The tramp pointed with a battered shoe at a carrier-bag beside the gatepost. 'Yes, I was given food,' he said and then, as if it was part of the same sentence, 'Don't do any mountaineering, will you?'

Nobody seemed able to think of an answer.

He spoke to Emma. 'I appeal to you,' he said, 'because women are always the restraining force when it comes to ventures. The mountain is very dangerous at this particular time of year.'

'We were just going for a walk on to the moor,' said Emma, edging round him so that he no longer stood in front of her.

'But during the course of your stay,' said the tramp, 'there will undoubtedly come a fine day when the mountain will look appealing. At this time of year, which is a time of sudden fogs and sudden squalls, it is not safe unless you are extremely familiar with the countryside.'

Emma by now had edged quite a few feet down the lane, so that, although he was still looking at her, the tramp was no longer within reasonable distance for a conversation. He made no move towards her. Peter wandered casually over to Emma and Michael was left alone.

'It's very kind of you to warn us,' he said pompously.

The tramp turned from Emma and smiled at him. He made no further attempt to speak.

'Good-bye,' said Michael, and walked purposefully towards the other two, who were now slowly making their way along the lane. When he caught up with them he looked back. The tramp, the brown-paper carrier-bag hanging from his hand, was walking towards the village. As Michael watched, he reached the bend in the lane, turned it without looking back and disappeared from sight.

'You two are a lot of help in times of crisis,' said Michael.
'Oh no! We're trapped.'

'I thought you wouldn't be pleased,' said Emma shyly.

Far ahead of them on the long straight track, at the point where it started out across the moors, was the unmistakable figure of Mrs White. She was walking so slowly that they couldn't possibly stay behind her but would have either to join her or to overtake her.

'This place is full of mad old men and women,' said Michael.

'He wasn't mad, though, was he?' said Peter doubtfully.

'We'd better start walking quickly now,' said Michael, who wasn't listening.

'Why?'

'If we overtake her at speed, we can just say "Hello" and be well past before she has time to engage us in conversation.'

'Walk normally,' said Peter. 'I don't know why you think she should want to bother to talk to us.'

But as they drew level with Mrs White she turned and looked at them, without slackening her slow, steady pace, and said, 'How nice of you to join me,' and automatically, though Michael scowled, all three fell into step with her. She walked with great determination and very upright, although she looked even older out of doors than she had within the protection of her cottage. They were now well on to the moor, the freshening wind full of the living smells of growing things, and the hedges had been replaced by dry-stone walls, very low, so that even Emma could see over them with ease.

'Is this the best way to go to the mountain?' said Peter.

Mrs White looked ahead along the straight path that so obviously led directly to the mountain, and then turned to Peter. 'Now what is it you really want to know?' she said.

Peter turned faintly pink. 'An old tramp just told us on no account to go up it,' he said.

'Did he?' said Mrs White. 'And how do you feel about that?'

'I'd like to climb it,' said Peter, 'and Mrs Myer didn't seem to think it was impossible. But the tramp said we mustn't.'

'And are you going to obey him?'

Michael broke in. 'When local people warn you about hazards it's only sensible to listen. He wasn't at all mad.'

'I'm sure he wasn't,' said Mrs White soothingly, 'and you're quite right to listen to warnings.'

The moor seemed very flat and wild now that they were well out on to it, though the grazing sheep were comfortingly solid.

'Are we walking too fast for you?' said Michael, his slight irritation at her company forgotten. He had suddenly noticed how thin and papery her hands looked against her dull grey coat and how evident were the strong bones of her handsome old face, so that he was uncomfortably aware of her delicacy.

'Not at all,' she said and then, mischievously, 'I have to get into training.'

'Training?' said Emma. She couldn't help laughing, but Mrs White didn't seem to mind.

'That's right. For when I go up the mountain myself.'

'Then you wouldn't tell people not to go up it?' said Peter.

'No, I wouldn't tell them that.'

'The tramp talked about sudden fogs at this time of year,' said Michael.

'Naturally one should *never* go up a mountain without checking the weather forecast very carefully,' said Mrs White primly. 'However, if you wish to go to the top of this mountain you are at least unlikely to get lost since you simply follow the path.'

'This path doesn't go straight to the top!' said Michael. 'It must stop at the foot.'

'Right to the top,' said Mrs White. 'Arthur's Way. That's because some people an exceedingly long time ago had the idea that the Holy Grail was hidden at the top and that Arthur's knights would have come this way in search of it. After all, the only honourable way to approach something as wonderful as that would be by a straight route. You wouldn't wander and ramble and creep up on it from behind – you would walk straight there with determination and dignity. Of course, no one ever found it – but here is the way.'

By now they had walked about half a mile and reached a stile at the side of the road. Mrs White sat down on it and stretched her legs out in front of her, smiling up at the mountain. Peter and Emma stood still and waited with her, and even to Michael it seemed quite natural to stand there while she rested, rather than to walk on.

Peter started to say something and then shook his head and frowned.

'Yes?' said Mrs White.

'I – keep getting a feeling that we're being watched,' said Peter, shrugging his shoulders to show how little weight he gave to his own remark.

'Quite possibly we are,' said Mrs White.

Although all three of them were facing in different directions, each looked instinctively and at once over his or her shoulder.

'You mean the sheep,' said Michael at last.

'Of course!' said Emma. 'Look at all those eyes!' She waved her arm at a group of six sheep who were just beyond the opposite wall. Instinctively they backed a few paces, without interrupting either their chewing or their staring.

'They could be forgiven for thinking that we're planning a trip to the mountain together,' said Mrs White dreamily, still looking up at it. 'They can't know that I'm not ready yet.'

There was complete silence for a moment or two.

'How – do you mean?' said Michael.

'It would take me an hour to reach the foot of the mountain,' said Mrs White, '– and three hours, perhaps four, to get to the top. And then, of course, one has to come back. I haven't the strength just now. But perhaps by the spring ...'

'But by the spring–' began Emma, and then stopped, looking rather confused. 'I mean, the mountain will be just as high in the spring.'

Mrs White reached out and patted her hand. 'You mean that by the spring I shall be even older,' she said. 'Well, I know that, but older doesn't necessarily mean weaker. It's all a matter of will and what one eats.'

'Isn't it almost as nice to look at the scenery from down here?' said Emma. 'I have an Uncle who says that scenery is ruined for him if he actually has to *walk* in it.'

'It would be nice to try once again,' said Mrs White.

'To find the Holy Grail?' said Peter.

Michael and Emma looked at him with surprise, thinking he was humouring her and doing it rather clumsily. But he was serious.

'I don't believe that was ever really there,' said Mrs White.

'Then what?'

'Listen,' said Mrs White. 'If I tell you a true story, will you tell me whether or not you accept it? Particularly you, Michael? There was once a witch-doctor in the African bush who had a very specific way of treating his patients for rheumatism, lumbago and general backaches. He would put on his headdress, naturally, and he would chant incantations, of course, because that was what was expected. But his basic instructions were to go and wallow in a particular mud-pool. When missionaries and doctors reached his village to try and dispossess him, they laughed at all his mumbo-jumbo and gradually managed to win the younger natives over to their way of thinking, medically speaking at least, with pills and injections. But the fact remained that nothing cured the rheumatics like a jump into that mud-pool, and the doctors were forced to call the cure psychological and permit it to continue. For a long time the white men were too busy fighting disease – much of which they had brought with them, I might add – to ponder on this miracle cure. Then one day when there was, I suppose, more time, someone had the bright idea of analysing the mud in the pool. They discovered it was fed by the warm waters of a mineral spring and was the equivalent of an extremely strong sulphur bath. It was, in a very real and physical sense, the perfect treatment for aches and pains. Do you believe that story, Michael?'

'Sounds quite sensible to me, yes.'

'So you believe the witch-doctor was right when he referred to the mud as having magical properties?'

'Well, to him they must have seemed magical because he wouldn't understand the way the thing was working.'

'And yet he knew it *did* work,' pursued Mrs White, 'and

he knew exactly how to use it for the best. So do you accept that that pool was magic?'

'In the sense in which you are using the word, I do,' Michael conceded suspiciously.

'Hm,' said Mrs White. 'Well, somewhere on top of the mountain is a magical spring. Shall we walk a little farther? It's too cold to sit about here any longer.'

They began to move slowly and steadily forward again.

'How do you know about the spring?' said Michael conversationally, because the others were stolidly silent.

'Because I found it – a great many years ago, when I was young. I was walking up there by myself and I found it. It flows over some rocks and then into a gully where it disappears underground. As far as I have ever been able to discover, it doesn't appear above ground again until it reaches the sea. I drank from it, because one gets hot climbing mountains, and mountain streams are very cool and pleasant. That was when I realized there was something very special about it. I was refreshed beyond all possible expectation. I felt more alive, more awake. When I came down again I talked about it, but people were fairly sceptical. So I said I'd take my father up there with me to see for himself. But I couldn't find it, and I've never found it since.'

They had reached a ridge, a crossroads. The tracks to left and right both led to farms, rambling buildings nearly a mile away in each direction. From this ridge it was possible to see how the valley undulated.

'I've said too much,' said Mrs White unexpectedly. 'Never mind. All the talk will be blown away by spring.'

Up to the crossroads the track they had been walking on had been gravelled. After the crossroads it was merely beaten earth.

'It becomes somewhat less visible as you progress along

it,' said Mrs White. 'But see how well marked it still is. See the menhir.' She pointed to the top of the next ridge and the standing stone that was there. 'When you reach that ridge,' she said, 'and stand this side of the stone, you will find that the tip of it points to the highest peak of the mountain.'

She turned to go back the way they had come, but Michael stood his ground, determined to walk further. Mrs White smiled. 'Have a nice walk,' she said.

'What did you mean,' said Emma, 'about thinking that we probably *were* being watched?'

Mrs White glanced quickly at Michael. 'There *are* things that I can't present in a wholly rational way,' she said, 'and I don't want to lose Michael's sympathy. If I have it, that is. But it is possible that one is not meant to know about the spring, or to find it again.'

'But what harm can there be?' said Emma. 'You just want to look at it – and perhaps drink from it again.'

'Oh, my dear child, not at all,' said Mrs White briskly, setting off for home with surprising speed. 'If I can get my hands on it I plan to divert it.'

5 AFTER tea they sat and wrangled rather dispiritedly by the fire. They were alone in the house because the Myers had gone to a special meeting of the local Preservation Society which had picked up a rumour of a road-widening scheme at a dangerous corner in the village. The possibility that the 1·5 per cent of summer visitors who were regularly damaged at that corner might escape unscathed worried the villagers less than the probability that a rather fine Elizabethan house would be destroyed.

'But what would we all do if we were at *home*?' said Emma at last, quite unable to get rid of the scratchiness in the atmosphere.

'Read a book,' said Peter, and he replaced the glass float, which for the last ten minutes had been reflecting his own face back at him, and went and crouched in front of the bookcase, looking vaguely for the folklore book Michael had accused him of reading on the first evening. As he had only used the book as a means of being left in peace, he couldn't immediately recognize it again.

'I'd read, too,' said Michael, not moving from Mr Myer's fireside chair, 'but those books don't look very appealing and I didn't bring anything with me. And there isn't a television, and I haven't seen any signs of a radio, and I don't want either of you to tell me your life-histories, so what's left?'

'Here it is,' said Peter, sitting on the floor against the book-case.

'What?'

Peter put the book on the floor and got down to it in earnest, on elbows and knees.

'It's quite a good one,' he said, drawling the way people do when they are reading one thing and saying another and what they are reading is the more interesting of the two. 'It's divided up into quite small areas so that you can just read up on the bit you're in ... It doesn't go into much detail, though, and we know all this already – going mad on the mountain overnight – and the Grail – and the hanged man at the corner ...' He leafed his way on through the pages.

'Well, someone's happily settled for the evening at least,' said Michael, and went to look along the shelves for himself. There were only about fifty books to choose from and none of the titles attracted him. Emma stretched and yawned and accepted the fire's flames as her entertainment for the evening.

'I wonder if these books are the Myers' or Mrs White's,' said Peter. 'This guidebook's good.'

'What does it say?' Emma asked politely.

Peter read on.

'I think this is the Myers',' said Michael. ' "Hydrangeas require a great deal of water, a fact which may easily be deduced from their name," you will be glad to know. Wow, there's an exciting evening's reading here! All the way from Antirrhinums to Zinnias, I shouldn't wonder.'

Peter sat up straight and held his book in front of his eyes to read. Then he put it down on the floor again and sat cross-legged, bending over it. He was too excited to keep still.

'What does it say?' said Emma, with more interest.

Peter turned the page but the guidebook had gone on to some other part of the district, and he sighed.

'It's just various ideas about the straight track to the top of the mountain,' he said. 'Mrs White's idea about having to approach the Holy Grail properly is there. And then there's some idea that it might have been an extremely old path that was designed when you had to find your way by natural landmarks, and the peak of the mountain would have been used as a sighting point. You know how Mr Myer said that everyone's always directing you to places by the mountain? And apparently very old traders' tracks – I mean, so old that often there isn't even a path there nowadays – were marked by standing stones like the one on the moor. And then there's this idea about Dragon Power – you'd think Mrs White would have mentioned that.'

'What do you mean?' said Emma. 'I don't want any more creepy stories.'

'It's not creepy. It's great.'

'Can I see?' said Michael dubiously.

Peter passed him the book and pointed to the paragraph. Michael read it aloud. 'Yin and Yang, the negative and positive life-forces, were known in China as the Dragon Current. These forces travel in straight lines, the positive magnetic current travelling over high mountains, and the negative along the lower hills. The point of their crossing was thought to be a particularly favourable place. Sacred buildings were sited along these lines and there is strong evidence that such a system, now largely destroyed, existed throughout Britain, the way marked by standing stones and by man-made ponds and hill notches, visible for many miles. An ancient straight track is easily traceable on the map from Doghead Point at the end of the Bay, via St Anne's Church, known to be built on a pre-Christian religious site, to the peak of Knowle Hill. The latter half of the track, Arthur's Way, is still a public right of way.

'Gosh,' said Emma, who wasn't quite sure what she thought. 'They call it a hill – I thought it was a mountain.'

'So, do dragons actually stalk the route?' said Michael, snapping the book shut.

'No – it's just a force, a power. Don't you think that's great?'

'Well, I don't know,' said Michael. 'What happens if you walk along the Dragon Current's path? Do you get an electric shock, or what?'

'Oh, don't jeer at that, too,' said Peter wearily. 'There *are* forces on the earth, you know there are. Why shouldn't a sort of life-force flow in straight lines? There's something very satisfying about that straight path up to the mountain, I could easily believe there's something special about it.'

'Sorry,' said Michael, 'but it *is* a bit far-fetched and remote. And the Chinese do have a fixation about dragons, remember.'

'It's not the dragons that count, it's the power.'

'No wonder people climb the mountain so easily. Walk as far as the standing stone, plug in for a few moments and then WHOOF, straight to the top.'

Peter laughed reluctantly. 'It's great,' he repeated. 'I've

never thought about currents of life-force like that. Can we look on a map; do you suppose there is one here?'

'Come on, dreamer, snap out of it,' said Michael good-humouredly.

'I just want to see if it's as easily traceable as they say.'

'I know. I just mean there's a fold-out map in the back of the book you're holding. I would have thought it was fairly obvious.'

They put the book on the floor and used a ruler that Emma reluctantly fetched from Mr Myer's desk top.

It was almost exactly twelve inches along the map from the peak of Knowle Hill to Doghead Point. As the book had promised, the ruler lay exactly along Arthur's Way and then went across country, straight through the centre of the village and its church, and along the edge of the harbour to the Point itself.

'I see Arthur's Way. Where's the rest?' said Michael.

'Who is it who's always saying things are fairly obvious?' said Peter.

And it was true; it was quite easy to see that the ruler left Arthur's Way at the kink in the lane by a field gate, and, passing through St Anne's Church, made for Doghead Point along a public footpath.

'See?' said Peter.

'Yes, I see,' said Michael. 'I see what my inferior, round-lensed eyes tell me. There probably was a very old straight track along that route. But I don't see dragons fitting in.'

'Dragon *Power*,' said Peter softly. 'Yin, do you suppose? And Yang flowing across the top of Knowle Hill the other way, all along the mountain and over the high peak and on to the end of the range? Where do you suppose they meet?'

'At Mrs White's magic spring, no doubt,' said Michael.

'Of course! And look! And look at the haunted corner –'

'Oh, look, I didn't mean that *seriously* –'

'– because something went wrong. The path should follow the line of power, but it turns. I suppose someone enlarged their field once, or something. Think of a very old straight path and then someone makes it turn. Perhaps it would confuse the force, and the corner would become an unpleasant place.'

'I don't like that idea,' said Emma sharply.

'It's quite ridiculous,' said Michael.

'No, it's exciting.' Facing the fire and them, Peter's eyes gleamed. 'There is a power. It fits. I believe it. I think it ebbs and flows, like the seasons, and I think it's flowing now. Something's happening now. Don't you know that?'

'Like what?'

'There just *is* something,' said Peter. 'Why, every time I get on that path, do I want to go up the mountain?'

'Perfectly normal reaction,' said Michael. 'It looks nice up there, and not particularly high. Let's arrange to go, for goodness' sake, and get it over with.'

'But then the séance . . . and the tramp . . .'

'Peter! She's a pleasant old woman and he's a strange old man and they've both got some truly weird ideas. Don't let them get a grip on you so that you start believing all that stuff.'

'And out there, walking along with her today, didn't you feel sort of vulnerable?'

'I thought *she* looked vulnerable,' said Michael. 'She's quite an old bird to go galloping about like that.'

'I do think someone ought to try to persuade her not to walk so far,' agreed Emma. 'I have an Uncle who –'

'But when I said I thought we were being watched, she said we probably were. And you felt it, too, both of you.'

'It was the sheep,' said Emma.

'No, it wasn't. I didn't want to argue out there, but it

wasn't the sheep, don't you see, because I *knew* they were looking at me, and you only get that feeling if something you can't see is watching you. It wouldn't be sheep anyway, they're not wild enough.'

'Where do you come from?' said Michael.

'What?'

'You heard.'

'Leeds.'

'And have you lived there long?'

'I was born there.'

'Exactly. And I was born in London. And I know just how you feel. You go out into the country and on to open moorland and get a sort of exposed feeling. It can be nice and free or it can be overwhelming – it depends how you're feeling at the time, I suppose. You feel exposed and – visible – because you're used to being one of a crowd of other people all swallowed up by buildings and streets. And because you feel visible you start to think you're being watched. I do understand, and I did feel it, but that's all it is – really.'

'You think that's all it is – I think something else,' said Peter. 'We'll just have to wait and see who's right. What I know is that the whole area, the fields, the mountain, the birds, particularly the starlings, everything, was watching us because we were with her and because of what she was saying. She said that "they" could be forgiven for thinking we were planning a trip now – and she said that her words would be gone by springtime when she hopes to make the trip again. Don't you see – by then, everything will have changed, new leaves, new grass, birds busy nesting. And so much is happening in the spring, always, that she may be able to sneak off, whereas now the countryside is just waiting, as it always does in the autumn, and because it's only waiting it's free to observe.'

60

'Oh lordy, lordy boy,' said Michael. 'You surely are in a bad way.'

'Everybody gets ideas like that,' said Emma, sitting straight and serious, with her hands in her lap as usual. 'But they're just ideas.'

Peter turned on her, almost angrily. 'You want to believe him,' he said, 'because it sounds safer. But really you believe me.'

PETER closed Mrs White's front gate carefully behind him and started up the path. He was glad to see the glow of light through her sitting-room curtains: it was only half past eight but he had been afraid she might go to bed early. Emma had said, 'Don't go now, she'll be in bed.' She had also said, 'The Myers'll be back any minute,' which had seemed a totally irrelevant objection to Peter, and, 'You won't get a straight answer from her about anything. You *think* she answers you, then you find you're just as confused but about something else.' Michael had said, 'All right, I grant you she may be right about a lot of things, but just remember, will you, that they're only *her* ideas and opinions. If they're a bit odd, don't swallow them whole, like that Dragon Power myth – just weigh them up a bit.'

When Peter had gone, Emma said, 'I thought you liked her better now.'

Michael banged the books about on their shelves. 'Yes, I like her. She *can* talk a lot of sense. But he'll swallow *anything* at the moment. He's got no intellectual discrimination at all.'

'That sounds pompous. Anyway, what does it matter?'

'It matters because it annoys me to see somebody seizing on any weird idea that comes along, without *thinking* about it. Dragon Power!'

Mrs White settled Peter by the fireside and said that indeed she had heard of the *lung-mei*, or dragon paths, in China. 'I could lend you books on it,' she said, 'if you're interested. And books which talk about old straight tracks all over Britain, too. Is that what you want?'

'I don't know,' said Peter. 'I want to climb Knowle Hill. I thought my wanting might be to do with the power.'

'It might.'

'But then – being warned not to . . .'

'I've told you that you must check on the weather. By nine o'clock on any morning at this time of year I would be able to tell you whether you are safe from fogs or not. In the summer, happy family groups trudged up, and down again, with monotonous regularity.'

So Peter explained about the séance. 'DGR and then DNGR,' he said, 'could only mean DANGER. And the message was for me.'

Mrs White laughed at him. 'Of course it was for you,' she said.

Of all the people who might have laughed at him for worrying about the séance – the strangeness of which had not been far from his mind – he wouldn't have thought that Mrs White would be one. 'Why is it funny?' he said.

63

'No, it isn't funny,' agreed Mrs White, nursing the black cat which was temporarily in a passive and affectionate mood, and looking – because of the firelight and the cat and because of her penchant for 40-watt lightbulbs – rather more witch-like than he would have thought possible. 'I'm only surprised that you don't understand. I would have thought ... Oh well. You did it, Peter, so naturally you addressed yourself.'

'No! I didn't do it. Really I didn't.'

'Don't you know how it works? Oh well, why should you, after all? The body heat from the fingers laid on the glass gradually warms the air trapped inside it. Warm air rises, yes? So the glass is now balanced on a cushion of air. It is only lifted by an infinitesimal amount – you won't see it rise like a hovercraft – but because it is on a cushion of air it can glide across the table far more easily than could a glass that one simply set on the table and began pushing around deliberately. Given the easy manœuvrability of the glass, the letters it selects are determined by the strongest force present. In this case it would have been you – partly because I believe you are a Piscean, are you not? – yes, I thought so – and so are very receptive to this sort of thing – and partly because you have the mountain on your mind. You feel a pull to climb it that is more than the normal urge to explore new territory. Because you don't quite understand the pull, you are nervous of it and resisting it. I don't mean that you controlled the glass physically – I mean that you were, by chance, generating the strongest emotional force among those present at that time, and so what was in your subconscious came out. And that was "The mountain is dangerous, Peter, don't go up it.' You want to go up it and you want an excuse not to.'

Peter sat quietly.

'Why else do you suppose the message was addressed to

you? Why did you know at once, instinctively – although you tell me that the glass was moving at tremendous speed – that it spelt "Do Try To Read"? You wanted them all to see that you had been told not to go. You wanted to be stopped. You didn't know you were doing it – I promise you that – but you were, and that is why this is a very dangerous and silly game to play unless one understands it. Suppose one of the players really believes that the glass brings messages from – what? – the "spirit world" – which are unalterably true. And suppose he is scared at the thought and sits down in a panic and thinks, "It may tell me I'm going to die soon or become incurably ill." If his is the strongest force present – and if he is frightened it probably will be – the glass will spell out a message of doom for him, straight out of his own mind. And he will believe it. And out of his fear and shock he may very well make himself ill. The human mind has enormous powers for good or evil. People can generate apparently supernatural occurrences out of their own minds, and not even know they have done it, and be afraid of their own creations. This is why it is so important to have a great deal of common sense and a very healthy respect for what one doesn't understand.'

When the Myers returned they were a little concerned to find that Peter was out, but at the same time they didn't feel he could come to much harm three doors up the lane.

Mr Myer grumbled quietly about the Preservation Society's meeting being a waste of time. 'All talk and no do,' he said. 'It was a wonderful meeting,' said Mrs Myer. 'The chairman and his wife invited us over for dinner next week.' 'Haven't even got their facts straight,' said Mr Myer. 'Aren't even sure, yet, that that worm-eaten frontage *is* to come down.' 'And,' said Mrs Myer exuberantly, 'I am to address the W.I. on the difficulties of adjusting to a new environment. I was asked during the coffee-break.' 'That lot,' said Mr Myer, 'couldn't work out how to preserve a dried prune.'

'Now, as soon as Peter comes in,' said Mrs Myer, 'we'll all have a cup of something hot and I'm going to make some cheese scones to fill up any gaps. Come and help me, Emma.'

'We've eaten,' said Emma.

'I know, but I remember being young,' said Mrs Myer archly. 'It's a long time till breakfast.' She shepherded Emma into the kitchen ahead of her.

'Must have been a greedy child, my wife,' said Mr Myer, sinking into his chair and closing his eyes.

'So you painted all four of them,' Peter was saying to Mrs White.

'Yes. They're not very good, I know, but I wasn't very much older than you are now and I've never been much of an artist.'

'You painted *the* spring?'

'Yes. Only from memory.'

'Who was the man in the fourth picture?'

'Someone I met once.'

To his annoyance, Peter felt the wall growing up between them that he had sensed before. There were things one didn't ask, things one didn't talk about, even if one couldn't see why they should be taboo. Now, while he was with her, he could feel it, he could feel that he mustn't ask any more – but he knew that once he had left, still wanting to know certain things, he would not be able to recall the feeling of restraint and would kick himself for not having fired off a few straight questions.

'Emma thought it might be a painting of your husband,' he said with an effort.

'Did she? I hadn't met my husband when I painted that.' She smiled, she stroked the cat, she was as warm and friendly as ever, but she had said her say and she was waiting for him to go.

'The Myers'll be wondering about me, I'd better get back,' he said obligingly. 'Don't disturb the cat, I'll let myself out.'

At the sitting-room door, he turned back. 'Thank you for explaining the séance,' he said.

'Are you happier about that now?'

'Yes. Thank you.'

Peter walked back in the dark. The séance explained, it still remained for him to understand the pull exerted on him by Knowle Hill, which he was intensely aware of even when he was indoors. He hurried down the lane, feeling for some reason like a conspirator who mustn't be seen returning from his secret meeting. In the tree beside the Myers' gate, a starling fidgeted and talked in its sleep. Peter ran indoors.

Mrs Myer arranged the three of them around the scrubbed kitchen table with over-buttered cheese scones and hot milk, and went into the sitting-room to try and extract from her husband a promise that he would attend with her the dinner party to be given by the Chairman of the Preservation Society.

'Mrs W. can't have reassured you all that much if a bird in a tree made you jump,' said Michael.

'It was just that they're usually out of sight at night – and it was at the gate, almost as if it was keeping a sort of watch ...'

'They've got to sit somewhere at night, poor beggars. And starlings are very common birds. It would have been almost odder if you hadn't seen one.'

'I feel a bit sick,' said Emma. The hot milk they got rid of down the sink easily enough. The scones they tried to eat, but after a cooked breakfast, a large lunch and an ample tea they couldn't cope. In the end they crumbled up three of the scones and swilled them down the sink – leaving three still on the plate because Michael said that if they got rid of all of them she'd make more next time.

Then Peter explained in detail about the séance. Michael was rather impressed.

'I didn't think it would be scientific enough for you,' said Peter.

'It's a lot better than it might have been. And I like the bit about common sense. So, look, are you going to overcome your subconscious fears and are we going to go up this wretched mountain?'

'And look for the spring, you mean?' said Peter.

'Why not? Good deed for the day. Anyway, a walk's more interesting if you've got a project.'

'But won't it be butting in?' Emma. 'Won't she mind us looking for her spring?'

'Mind?' said Michael. 'I think she's been angling for us to offer since she met us, don't you?'

'I thought so,' said Peter. 'Although there's something that doesn't want us to go. Something's watching and I still think it's the starlings. *Why* didn't I ask her more about that instead of being so anxious about the séance?'

'So we'll ask Mrs Myer for a picnic,' said Michael ignoring him. 'Oh lord, I suppose we'll need a mule to carry it. And then call in tomorrow at nine en route for a weather report and to find out where she wants the spring diverted *to*, in the very unlikely event that we do find it.'

At that point Mr Myer came into the kitchen to suggest that bedtime might be upon them all.

'Planning a trip up the mountain?' he said. He looked anxious, which was unusual for him.

Michael said that they were.

'I wouldn't,' said Mr Myer. 'I really wouldn't.'

'It isn't high,' said Michael, 'we've looked on the map –

you walk and scramble, that's all. It's not North-Face-Of-The-Eiger stuff.'

'People get lost on mountains,' said Mr Myer. 'Fog – and things – Don't be deceived by the name. It *is* a small mountain, not a hill.'

'We'll check the weather. And we'll follow the path. It'll be as good as unrolling a ball of string behind you in a forest. We *can't* get lost.'

'We're responsible for you while you're here,' said Mr Myer.

'It'll be all right,' said Michael. 'We'll do it sensibly.'

Mr Myer looked unhappy. He didn't forbid them, he just looked unhappy.

'I'm glad you're so confident everything'll be all right,' Peter said to Michael, as the three of them made their way upstairs. 'But then, why shouldn't you be? I'm the only one who believes we're being opposed.'

Emma woke up at about three o'clock in the morning, aware that there was something in her room. It was a clear night, but the almost full moon was shining on the other side of the house and her bedroom was quite dark.

In the fireplace something seemed to sigh. Emma lay quite still, holding her breath. She didn't think she was going to be able to scream.

There was a scratching noise on the floor, nearer than the sigh. It was a small room and the fireplace was not far from the bed. Her heart was pounding so loudly that she couldn't listen properly. She breathed as shallowly as she could and turned her head very slowly to look towards the sound, although she knew it was too dark to see what was there.

It seemed to be something small. Something small and awful was creeping towards her across the floor. Surely

Michael would hear the scratching and scrabbling through the wall. But she knew he wouldn't. It was too soft.

Terrible visions came into her mind of something that would claw its way slowly up the side of her bed. Something that would have small, dry, cold hands – that would creep towards her – and touch her –

To her own amazement, as well as everyone else's in the house, she let out a sizeable scream.

When she had screamed once she had to scream again and again. It was as if it had been smelling her out before, but now that she had made such a noise it would know where she was and come straight for her.

They had to come quickly with light. They had to come very quickly.

Michael burst in first, with Peter a couple of yards behind him. In the second before they switched on the light, something brushed past Emma's head, and this final terror stopped her screaming.

Then Michael switched on the light and he could see that she was sitting bolt upright in bed, her normally rosy face white, and her hands protecting her throat. A little beyond her, on the end of her bed, crouched the confused and still slightly stunned bird that had slipped down the chimney. The two boys went over to it.

'Let me,' said Peter. 'My father used to keep pigeons.' He picked it up and examined it gently, pulling its wings out to full span and looking at its legs. 'It isn't hurt,' he said.

Mr and Mrs Myer, from their floor below, came into the room not half a minute after the two boys.

'It's just that a bird fell down the chimney and gave her a fright,' said Michael. 'It's all right.'

Mrs Myer was shocked. Not about the bird, which in any case seemed to be all right, but at Emma's reaction. Solid, sensible Emma was white and shaking and very nearly hysterical. Mrs Myer's mind went back to conversations about the haunted lane, to the séance – to times when Emma, sitting calmly still – or was it rigid? – had held her own hand in her lap.

'Poor little girl,' she said quietly. 'Come on. We're going down to make a cup of tea, and we'll leave all the lights on all night if you like.' She helped Emma, who hardly seemed to know how to manage it herself, into her dressing-gown.

Peter opened the window and put the bird on the sill. It stood for a moment or two, shuffling its wings, and then flew easily to the nearest tree. Mr Myer, looking helpless, withdrew from the scene. Peter closed the window behind the bird.

Mrs Myer led Emma to the door. 'I should have realized you didn't like all this spooky nonsense,' she said. 'You look so calm ... just like my mother ... I should have realized. Come on, dear.'

'It was a starling,' said Peter. 'Does this mean we'll all be too ... tired to go tomorrow?'

'Oh, I don't think a starling with a bad sense of direction need worry us unduly,' said Michael.

Emma turned round at the door. 'I shall be all right,' she said shakily.

'We'll see, we'll see,' said Mrs Myer, and led her down the stairs.

7 IT was so sunny and bright the next morning that Michael, who woke up first, and who slept in the middle bedroom, was prompted to bang on the walls at both sides and announce the fact.

'It's the landing light, only,' Emma called back. 'It's been on all night.'

'Wake up!' said Michael. 'It's genuine sunlight.'

It was well after eight and a tremendous commotion seemed to be going on outside at the back. They could hear the Myers' voices as well.

Suddenly Mrs Myer's voice rose, clear and high, through the hubbub. 'It's a *plague* of starlings,' she said.

Michael, fully dressed, Emma, in her dressing-gown and Peter, with his shirt hanging out, met on the landing, looked at each other and ran quickly downstairs.

'Come and look!' called Mrs Myer, hearing them. 'Come and look at the *armies* of starlings!' Her voice came from the kitchen and the commotion, now more clearly recognizable as being made by birds, from outside the back door. They went into the kitchen, Peter first.

'Look!' said Mrs Myer again. The Rowan tree, between the kitchen window and the back door, seemed to be a tree of birds, heaving and tugging, squawking and shoving, each one trying to cram as many of the fat red berries down its throat as possible.

'I should have harvested the berries yesterday if I wanted to use them,' said Mrs Myer. 'But I somehow can't bring myself to shoo the birds away now. I feel the berries are for *them* rather than for us. Anyway, I don't think they'd go.'

She turned to the stove. 'Breakfast in three minutes,' she said. 'And do wrap up warmly, with lots of sweaters, if you're really going out for the day.'

A starling, its beak stained horribly red by the feast, raised its head and frowned into the kitchen. Then it shrugged its wings with a sharp click and went back to its meal.

'All a matter of country routine,' said Michael to Peter. 'Birds eat berries. Very healthful and natural.'

Michael really wanted to set out before nine o'clock but somehow there were a great many delays. After the starlings there was breakfast to get through. Then Mrs Myer took the boys aside in turn and urged them to look after Emma. 'She looks solid,' she explained several times, 'but she isn't. The calmer she looks the more frightened she is. Will you remember that?'

After that, Mr Myer began to fidget and at last insisted on lending Michael a compass. It was rather an attractive, old compass, small, and designed to be worn on a watchchain. In the end, Emma agreed to take charge of it, adding it to the

St Christopher she already wore round her neck. Next, Mrs Myer refused to pack the picnic, which she was putting into Mr Myer's new and unused rucksack, without supervision from all three – did they like this, did they like that? And, finally, Mr Myer wanted to do an 'equipment check' – had they a map? etc.

Peter, irritated beyond irritation, retired to the sitting-room alone, sat down and lifted the glass weight into his lap, as he had done several times since the first afternoon, always without result. He warmed the stone in his hands, looked into the float, and gradually relaxed. Just like the first time, the picture was there before he knew it. He gazed at it dreamily, unable to understand what it was and at the same time knowing that if he focused sharply on the image it would go. He saw blackness and some points of light that glimmered. He waited for them to form into something, but they did not change. He counted them. There were twelve. Three in a row, then one slightly lower and out on its own to the right. Then below that and to the left four in a wavy line; and below them again, and still farther over to the left, the last four formed a rough square. He noticed all this and yet still none of it made sense to him.

'If you're communing with Mrs White you can tell her we're just coming to see her,' said Michael in the doorway. Peter's eyes snapped into sharp focus and the glass cleared. He got up with a sigh and put it back on the mantelpiece. He had an odd feeling that he would like to take it with him, almost for comfort.

'I didn't see her,' he said.

'You mean you did see something?'

Peter went over to Mr Myer's desk, picked up a pencil, found a used envelope and made dots on the back of it in, as nearly as he could remember, the pattern he had seen. Michael looked.

'The silly thing is,' said Michael, 'that it looks vaguely familiar, but I really don't know why ... Is that all you saw? Just black spots?'

'No, white spots on black. Shiny spots. Like – like rain-drops on – oh – black velvet – I don't know.'

'Stars!' said Michael. 'You're transferring images again. That little picture upstairs of the mountain with the stars shining behind it. They're arranged like this.'

Peter looked at him for a moment. 'Yes, you're right,' he said slowly. 'I hadn't remembered. But the stars I saw shone; the ones in the painting were flat dabs of white.'

'So you improved on art!'

'All right. I suppose I really did do it,' said Peter. 'Like I did the séance. Though I still can't work out how I managed to get Mrs White's face the first time ...'

'Never mind. Can't we hurry up and go? It's half-past nine and we're never going to get away. Fuss, fuss, fuss about food – fuss, fuss, fuss about clothes – fuss, fuss, fuss about Emma ...' He crossed the hall into the kitchen and Peter, following him, heard him start the same sentence all over again, from 'Can't we hurry up and go?'

And eventually they did, at about ten o'clock. Michael helped Peter on with the heavy rucksack. 'An hour each,' he said.

'Come on,' said Emma, standing halfway down the path and screwing up her eyes against the sun.

'Now let's go and surprise Mrs White with the revelation that we're going on her Quest!' said Michael.

Mrs White observed their approach up her path through her owlish glasses, which, as always, she had removed by the time they reached the front door, and then confronted them with the – to Michael anyway – oddly disquieting fact that she already knew they were going.

'The day is perfect,' she said approvingly, leading the expedition into her sitting-room. 'And here is a large-scale map, with the area where I found the spring clearly marked. And here, you see,' as they bent obediently over the map which had awaited them on the table under the window, 'is the spring which feeds the reservoir from which comes water for the whole village. I am convinced that the two are very close together – and I want you to divert the magic spring into the other.' She beamed at them. 'Don't you think water like that should be available to everybody?'

Michael became silent and drew back a little. His bossy confidence was gone and he felt like a child again. 'This is, all the time, why she wanted to meet us,' he thought. 'We *are* ingredients in a recipe.' He had a sudden urge to say, 'We're not going after all.' They had been led towards this – Quest – so inevitably, he now saw, that he wanted to change things just to prove he could. But he didn't. He thought that the reason he didn't was because it would have been rather childish – and, what was more, a clear case of cutting off one's nose to spite one's face, because he wanted to go.

Peter was saying something about taking a shovel, or some means of shifting earth, but Mrs White said that wouldn't be necessary. 'Just a rearrangement of large stones,' she said with assurance.

She folded up the map and gave it to Peter. And then she picked up her owlish glasses from the table under the window and gave them to Emma. 'Take these with you,' she said. 'I didn't tell you this before, but in the spring I found a very small nugget of gold. In fact I never told anybody at all – I didn't want them tearing at the mountain – and for the same reason I don't want you to tell anybody either. But I had the frames of these glasses made from the gold, and I have an idea, which may be mistaken, that there is some kind of magnetic attraction between this metal and any that may still be up there, at the spring. Do you understand? I believe you might use the glasses as a kind of divining rod.' Emma held out her hand for them. 'But Emma, don't look through them, will you?'

'Why not?' said Michael, from his retreat at the side of the room, where he was fingering the sharp leaves of a spider-plant.

'Because you should never look through other people's glasses. You could hurt your eyes.'

As soon as he had the map, which seemed to be his responsibility, Peter turned away from the others and continued his examination of the fascinatingly overfull room. It was an examination he had begun during their first visit, and he felt he would never complete it. He moved over to the sideboard for a closer look at a Chinese puzzle: an intricately carved ivory ball which was contained within a larger and equally intricately carved ivory ball, which was contained within ... and so on. It fascinated him and made him feel fidgety at the same time.

He looked away from it and his eye was caught by the large astrological chart that hung on the wall directly in front of him. It was circular, and divided into twelve segments by fine black lines. In each segment there were words and pictures and diagrams, all finely and beautifully executed and all quite alien to Peter who had never come across anything like it before.

The segment at the top of the chart attracted him the most because the drawing was the right way up, whereas all the others slanted and the one at the bottom was actually upside down. It showed a robed figure carrying an elegantly shaped gourd from which he seemed to be pouring water on to the ground. The inscription alongside it was hard to read because of the flamboyant handwriting, but he made it out at last: 'Aquarius, the Water Bearer, Pouring forth

Knowledge.' And next to the inscription, almost at the centre of the segment, there was a diagram. While he stared at it, Emma stared in equal surprise at the spectacles Mrs White had put into her hand.

They were strange-looking, and fragile for their size. The lenses were large and round and the frames made from a very narrow thread of plain gold. But the ear-pieces were delicately carved to look as if two slender serpents twisted their way around each one.

'Snakes,' said Emma dubiously.

'The staff of Hermes,' said Mrs White. 'Or Mercury, if you prefer. A god of roads and paths, among other things.'

Then she disturbed Michael still further by approaching each one of them, putting her hands on their shoulders and kissing them on both cheeks. It was affectionate but formal, and Michael thought again, 'We don't have to go.'

'You don't have to go,' said Mrs White, smiling at them from her front door. 'But I expect you will, won't you?'

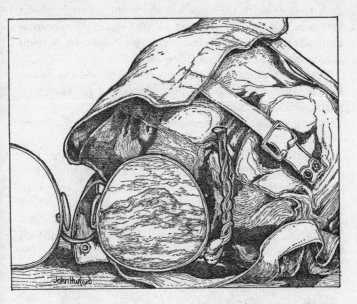

THE gravel of the lane crunched under their feet. The sun shone in their faces with surprising warmth, though the air was cool and clear. Peter plodded, because of the rucksack, but Emma danced and Michael kicked stones and laughed aloud. 'Great!' he said. 'It's great!'

'You know those stars?' said Peter. 'I've found out what they are.'

'Oh?' said Michael.

'On that chart in Mrs White's room. They're the constellation of Aquarius.'

'Oh?' said Michael again. 'So?'

'So nothing. I just thought you'd be interested.'

Emma swung Mrs White's spectacles from one hand. Michael had offered to pack them carefully in the rucksack for her, with the map, but she wouldn't let him. She said they were too fragile and might be crushed. The sunlight caught them and struck sparks of light from them which cut through the bright morning like signal flashes.

Their path dipped and the houses behind and the mountain before vanished from view. There was so much sun, such fresh air, such a sense of release, that Michael wanted to turn cartwheels, but he wasn't sure he could remember how, so he limited himself to singing.

The starlings, who had watched their departure with interest, had elected to stay with the still-abundant Rowan berries. There were birds, but not many, and all the sheep were in the distance. A robin considered them for a time from a dry-stone wall and then flew away as they drew level with it. An army of plovers feeding in a ploughed field seemed to be uneasily aware of their presence and Michael waited, acid comments at the ready, for Peter to say something about them; but he said nothing.

'"Hey ho, hey ho, it's OFF to work we go!"' sang Michael.

The nearest plovers rose in the air with thin despairing cries, circled the field and landed on the far side.

'" It's a long WAY to Tipperary!"' sang Michael.

'You go in for the really modern stuff, don't you?' said Peter.

'It's almost hot when you're walking,' said Emma.

Although the sun was well clear of it, and shining full in their faces, the mountain, being in the east, presented a shadowy front to them and only its highest points were touched with light.

The ground rose gradually, towards the crossroads, and Emma turned back to admire the view. 'Look!' she said approvingly.

'Very picture postcardy,' said Michael.

'It's odd,' said Emma, 'that they choose the best and most attractive views for picture postcards, but when you say that, I know you're being rude.'

They reached the crossroads, where the tracks to left and right led to the two big farms and, beyond the southerly farm, to the convent. Now they were high enough to see the sea itself, shining in the bay, and Mrs White's house, and the Myers' house, and indeed the whole village.

'Village church straight in front of us down there,' said Michael, turning on his heel. 'And the standing stone straight behind us.'

Emma swung the glasses and little swords of sunlight stabbed out from them.

'She's signalling to the dragon,' said Michael.

'Yes, it's funny,' said Emma, 'I do feel as if I'm signalling.' She swung the glasses in an arc around her head. 'I think it's because the flashes seem to go such a long way. I bet they can see them from the village, if anyone's looking.' She swung the gleaming glasses back the other way. 'I wonder what I'm saying?'

'Don't!' said Peter.

'Why? Is the dragon abroad?' said Michael.

'She'll break them if she plays with them like that.'

'No I won't,' said Emma. 'They are fine, aren't they?'

'Here, it's your turn with the rucksack,' said Peter to Michael. 'While we're changing over, let's put the glasses away safely.'

'No!' said Emma. 'They're beautiful. I like looking at them.'

'Well, they're blinding me,' said Peter. 'You keep flashing them in my eyes and all I can see now are blobs of colour.'

'Look the other way, then,' said Michael. 'Sun's just beginning to creep down the mountain.'

Peter slipped the rucksack from his shoulders and lowered it to the ground. 'Look at the sheep walking straight up the mountain,' he said, his attention caught by the distant lumpy shapes. 'It's a wonder they don't break their silly legs.'

Emma still faced the way they had come, with her back to the boys. She hooked the ear-pieces of the glasses over her ears so that the lenses were under her chin. She knew that she only wanted to put them on because she had been told not to, but at the same time she couldn't believe that looking through them for one short moment could damage her eyes.

'I expect they do,' Michael said. 'I expect there's a regular Picturesque Happening around here as a shepherd carries his lame sheep home.'

Emma wished she had a mirror with her. She thought she would like to put the glasses on and just take a quick look at herself, all wise and important behind the owlish lenses and with the serpents, of which she had grown rather fond, writhing across her temples.

Peter picked up the rucksack and guided Michael's arms through the straps. 'Let's eat it all *soon*,' said Michael, as he took the weight. 'It'll dislocate my spine.'

Emma gave up the struggle and put the glasses on, properly.

To her surprise everything did not blur and ripple as she had expected it to. She continued to look at the village and she saw it as clearly as before. The only difference was that all around the outside of her vision the golden frames glowed in the sun. She was about to ask the other two how she looked, but as she turned she saw that something was moving towards them along the track from the southern farm.

It was approaching quite slowly and quite silently. And

the thought came into her mind, 'It's the dragon ... I've conjured up the dragon.'

She forgot that she had meant to take the glasses off almost as soon as she had put them on. The boys were still talking about sheep and it was quite obvious that they hadn't seen the apparition that was coming to engulf them; but she couldn't say anything, she just stood and stared as it moved steadily nearer. One side of it was dark, like black light – if such a thing should be possible – and it flickered; the other side was pale and still.

And then, in a moment, her eyes made sense of what they saw – and she was frightened because it was normal and yet abnormal. What she saw was two nuns, progressing steadily towards the crossroads. They were carrying collecting-boxes and had presumably stopped off at the farm en route from the convent to the village. But the reason they had looked so extraordinary, and had appeared to be one creature, was that each was surrounded from the top of her head, right down her body, and even under her feet as she lifted them from the ground, by a kind of light. The light around one of the nuns was still and pale golden in colour, like the sun early on a spring morning. But the light around her stern-faced sister was black, and moved – writhed almost. The golden light was all of a piece, but the dark light seemed to be made up of hundreds of little separate facets. And as the nuns drew closer still, Emma could see what those facets were – crucifixes – small, black, sharp crucifixes on which the body moved, twisted in pain; such pain! Emma's eyes filled with tears. She was aware that Michael said something, but she didn't hear what it was. She assumed that he had turned round from the mountain and was exclaiming in surprise at this extraordinary vision.

Then she noticed one more thing. Where the golden light

of the first nun came into contact with her companion's aura, the figure on the cross was stilled, was at peace, and in some places, where the bodies of the two nuns were closest, it dissolved away entirely, so that the crosses were empty, and light.

The sunlight reflecting from the frames of the owl glasses was all at once too bright and sharp to bear, and Emma took them off.

At that point the nuns drew level. The nun with the young-old face smiled a greeting with such warmth in it that all three children smiled back and Michael put some money in the collecting-box she carried. The nun with the sharp-featured, austere face acknowledged them also, but only with a slight inclination of her head, and with straight lips.

And, without the glasses, that was all that Emma saw. Two ordinary nuns.

Her head hanging, she folded the glasses in her hands, and then noticed that Peter was watching her.

'What do they do?' he said.

'What do you mean?' said Emma, as Michael unconcernedly watched the receding backs of the nuns, now making their slow and steady way towards the village.

Peter moved closer to her and held out his hand for the glasses, which she did not pass to him. 'I could see from behind that you had them on,' he said. 'The frames stick out beyond your face. And they glowed. I've never seen anything like it. They glowed as if they were red hot. What did you see?'

'Nothing.'

'Tell me.'

Emma glanced at Michael. 'I wasn't meant to look,' she said.

'Come on – what happened?' said Michael, interested at

last, and they both stood side by side and stared at her. So she told them.

Peter said. 'I thought it was something like that.'

'Why?'

'Just because she always watched us through them as we came up her path but never let us see her in them from close to.'

'You're dreaming,' said Michael.

'No. I saw. It was horrible.'

'Let me look.' He held out his hand. When Peter did that, it was a request. When Michael did it, it was more like an order.

'No.'

'How can I believe if I don't see?' said Michael.

'Oh, come *on*,' Peter said to him.

'We're not meant to,' said Emma. 'Suppose you looked at us. What you see could alter everything.'

'Please,' said Michael firmly.

'You may as well let him,' said Peter. 'It's the only way you'll convince him, and the damage has been done now, the secret is out.'

'Look,' said Michael. 'There's the perfect target.' A woman of about thirty was walking slowly down the farm track, the way the nuns had come, dragging behind her a push-chair with a child in it.

'Off to the village shops!' said Michael. 'Let me look at her through the glasses and I promise I won't look at either of you. Please, Emma.'

Emma didn't give him the glasses, but she allowed him to take them away from her.

Michael moved so that he had his back to the others but faced the 'target'. He put the glasses on.

The woman was pushing the child in front of her now, a fat, pink boy of about a year old. He held a switch with a few tattered leaves on it which he trailed on the path behind and entangled in the wheels below his chair.

Emma watched the back of Michael's head, haloed, almost, with the rays from the frames.

'Well?' said Peter.

Michael's voice was subdued. 'The baby's got pink,' he said. 'Iridescent. Like bubbles. But the woman's got – it's hard to say – like a fog, that sort of greyish-yellow fog you get in a city. Thick. But the thing is – the thing is, where her greyness touches the baby's pink bubble the bubble seems to absorb it and go dull. The back of his head has got a little cloud over it.'

The woman was by now near enough to see them quite clearly, and Michael took the glasses off and passed them behind his back to Emma. Nobody said anything and Emma cried without making any sound.

The baby dropped its switch rather listlessly and banged its hands on the arms of its pushchair. The woman plodded on, ignoring it. The nearside wheel of the pushchair went over a stone and it lurched. The baby let out a wail. They were now level with the children.

'Good morning,' said Michael.

The woman looked at him as if she was really too tired even to turn her head. 'Morning,' she said, on an outward sigh. Then she turned her back on them to follow the nuns down the long trail to the village. A continuous grizzle came from the baby.

'It's all right,' said Peter to Emma.

'We'll never look through them again,' said Michael.

'Oh, you're stupid!' said Emma unexpectedly. 'Don't you see that they only show up what's already there, the way a beam of sunlight shows up all the floating bits and pieces that are *always* in the air. Not seeing it won't help. It's always like that.'

'That's what I mean,' said Peter. 'It's all right. It's always like that and it's always *been* like that, and we survive. Being aware of it may even have a positive effect on us. And sometimes the nicer one is the stronger one, don't forget that. Don't worry about the baby ... by the time it's older it'll probably have surrounded itself with a wall of roses so thick it'll overcome her grey fog.'

Emma conceded a small smile.

'And it isn't *permanent*,' Peter went on. 'She may be grey smog today and yellow butterflies tomorrow.'

'Shall we have our coffee?' said Michael soberly. 'Don't you think we need it now?'

'No,' said Peter. 'We need a brisk walk. Let's get to the stone.'

They walked up the path towards the tall menhir. The sun was now well above the mountain and every ridge and rock was lit and golden so that its covering of brown and dying bracken was made rich and vital. The stone cast a long shadow. The sky was still incredibly clear and the moor as beautiful as it had been when, earlier, Michael had wanted to turn cartwheels; but it wasn't only the weight of the rucksack that dimmed his enthusiasm for such activity now. Emma mopped her eyes with her handkerchief. Peter walked ahead, fast.

'Just because you're not carrying the rucksack ...' said Michael.

'We're going to get up there,' said Peter.

'Yes, I know,' said Michael. 'I'm with you – honestly. But it *is* heavy. Funny. The sun's quite clear of the mountain now, but it doesn't seem as bright as it did.'

'Huh!' said Peter. 'Only because we're wrapped up in thick black auras of depression. And *why*? Nothing's changed.'

'Has for me,' said Michael quietly.

'Oh you,' said Peter, 'you're just slow to catch on, that's all. You're just a bit limited by an excess of common sense.'

The stone grew nearer and taller and they puffed as they crunched up the slope towards it. 'I suppose the north side of it is covered in moss,' said Michael irrelevantly.

'Come on, nearly there,' said Peter, as Michael began to unhook the rucksack from his shoulders.

'It's a bit dark and forbidding, isn't it?' said Emma.

The ground sloped so steeply towards it that they realized they were in fact walking on the very hem of the skirt of the mountain.

The stone was almost nine feet tall and about three feet wide – grey and pitted and so very ancient that it was almost alien.

'Base camp,' said Michael, and he slung the rucksack down in the long shadow. As it landed, a dark figure rose up from behind the stone and moved slowly round it to meet them.

EMMA honked like a frightened goose and Michael shouted, 'What were you hiding behind there for?'

The man was tall and slim and darkly bearded, dressed like a casual walker in jeans and a black jumper, and he leant his shoulder on the south side of the stone and observed them steadily through golden-brown eyes. When the old tramp was middle-aged he must have looked something like this, Emma saw.

'You leap to the conclusion,' said the man politely, 'that because I happened to be concealed by the stone I was hiding from you.'

'Why did you jump out at us?' said Michael.

'Why did you throw your belongings down with such force that I felt the ground move underneath me?'

'Come on,' said Michael to the others, 'let's keep moving.

We're behind schedule.'

'Ah, you walk to schedules, do you?' said the man. 'Where are you going?'

'That's nothing to do with you.'

'Don't go on up this way.'

'Does the mountain belong to you, then?' said Michael.

The man laughed ... and waited. It was very still. There was no wind and no trees to rustle if there had been. Along the valley a single bird called.

Peter said, 'It might only be a friendly warning ...'

'Yes, very friendly,' said the man.

Michael retrieved the rucksack from the shadow of the monolith, and began to walk around the stone and the man who seemed to speak for it.

'Not that way,' said the man, watching him.

'We happen to want to go up this way.'

'Of course. Straight tracks have great allure. It's an ancient magic. That's why you don't like to step on the cracks in paving-stones, the ones that cross your path. All lines, all ways should be straight.'

Emma put her hand to the back-pocket of her jeans where the glasses had their somewhat precarious resting place.

'Hundreds of people come this way every year,' said Michael.

The man pushed off from the stone with his shoulder so that he stood upright. He had a strong face, not unpleasant but rather austere. His clothes suited him simply because they were so weather-worn that they were quite unobtrusive and yet ... Emma thought she could picture him in a monk's robe. He was not old and yet, oddly, was not of this time. He would have looked right with a robe and a staff and a book. But whether this was really so, or whether she was affected by the proximity of the oddly powerful stone, which seemed to exist in its own time and not in theirs, Emma was not sure.

'But not you,' said the man. 'This is not for you, this venture.'

Emma brought the glasses round from behind her back and put them on. The frames did not glow and the man looked no different through their lenses than he had through her own eyes. He smiled at her. Then he laughed. Not unkindly. Emma took the glasses off. It was as if he had recognized them and refused their analysis.

'You can't stop us,' said Michael.

'Indeed I could. I could change your minds by returning to you what you give to me. If I do not accept the fear or the dislike you are directing at me, to whom does it belong? To you, I think. I would break you, I believe, with indignity – and you, little girl, with physical pain, or the fear of it; and you,' he looked at Peter, 'you with compassion – and that would be a pity because compassion is good and one does not wish to harm those who feel it. But I won't stop you. If you must go on, you go on. I tell you not to, that's all. I advise you not to, and I request you not to.'

'Come *on*,' said Michael, inching away and upwards, although he was quite obviously held by the steady eyes and the quiet voice which had something of a hypnotic quality about them.

'How do you know what we're doing?' said Peter, and Michael swung round and glared at him.

'She said,' said the man, 'that all the talk would be blown away by springtime. But it isn't springtime and she's sent you too soon. She's never sent anyone else before, she wanted to do it herself, but she has failed, year after year after year, and now she is thinking two things – that she may not have the physical strength to try again, ever, and that perhaps one can only find this thing once in a lifetime. She has sent you now in case she never again finds anyone willing.'

'Peter!' said Michael. 'Peter! Peter!' Peter turned at last to look at him. 'You always believed we were being opposed. What did you think? That we'd meet some kind of jaw-gnashing monster which would be so obviously evil that we'd run at once? That's childish! This man is far more subtle than that – but this is the opposition you knew would come. Why are you listening? Are we going to let ourselves be *talked* out of going?'

The man moved quickly towards Michael, as if he was going to catch hold of him, but as soon as he had Michael's attention he stopped. 'Why are you afraid to listen?' he said. 'You find me difficult to understand only because you think so rigidly. You can't decide if I'm Good or Bad and that worries you. You can't, can you?' He looked at Emma. 'You even resorted to those glasses to find out. But life is not so simple. There is no need for you to assume that because the old lady is undoubtedly good she is also right. Or that because I oppose her I am bad and wrong.'

'We can't argue with him,' said Michael. 'All we know is that he is against what we agreed to do. Therefore we ignore him.'

'Why?' said the man. 'Think. Is it so wrong to begin on a Quest you believe in and then to turn aside if you find you've made a mistake after all?'

'You see how clever he is?' said Michael. 'He knows if he said things against her, he'd turn us against *him*. So he says nice things about her but opposes what we want to do for her.'

'The old woman is good, and full of love,' said the man sadly, 'but misguided.'

'We go on!' said Michael, struggling farther away, almost

as if he was held back by some force. 'He can't stop us, we go on.'

Peter took Emma's hand and led her out of the stone's shadow and into the sun. 'Yes, all right,' he said. He looked at the man who had moved back to the stone and now leant on it again, as if he was tired. 'We go on.'

'Yes,' said the man. He sat down on the south side of the stone and watched them. Michael began to move faster, bending forward to compensate for the weight of the rucksack and the steep slope of the way. He didn't look back as Emma and Peter came up behind him.

They were all breathing heavily and careless feet were dislodging small stones which rattled back down the path for a few feet, but they heard the strong voice of the man quite clearly as he spoke to them from where he sat, many yards below them now.

'You cannot carry out someone else's Quest,' he said.

I0 THEY walked on up and they hardly spoke. Occasionally the very straightness of the way defeated them and Michael, who was ahead, led them away from the beaten-earth track so that they crossed a particularly steep section slantwise, across small boulders. The covering of earth and wiry grass was sparse, and the rock that was the mountain itself broke through its own thin skin in many places, offering firm footholds. They walked like city dwellers, carelessly, dislodging earth and small pieces of shale, allowing their feet to become temporarily wedged in crevices that a little care would have enabled them to avoid.

After a while they came to a tiny plateau, not more than twenty feet square, where they were faced by a sheer wall of rock about twelve feet high. Presumably the track led straight up the rock; certainly they could see that it continued where the land levelled off again.

'There are footholds,' said Peter dubiously, inspecting a few vertical fissures in the rock.

'No, we'll have to find a way round,' said Michael.

'If we lose the track we'll never find the spring.'

The mountain rose towards its crest in a series of undulations, and now that they were actually halfway up it was not possible to see the top at all. At the foot of each undulation they could look up and see the skyline, not far away, as if the summit was within fifteen minutes' walk, and then at the crest of each undulation they saw the beginning of the next. The mountain leant back, away from them, so that by looking down they could see how far they had come, but they had no way of judging how far they still had to go. The track was the only thing that gave them a specific sense of direction, and it was by now obvious that only if they followed it could they be sure of reaching the peak where the spring might be.

'We won't lose it,' said Michael irritably, 'but if you seriously think we can make it up that wall I really think you'd better look again.'

Instead, Peter looked back, for the first time, both ways along the valley and then straight down at the stone, tiny now, but somehow no less important in its isolation than when it had overshadowed them. There was nobody standing or sitting beside it and no sign of movement. 'He's gone,' said Peter.

Michael stood beside him and looked down. 'I wonder where,' he said. 'We can see so far – how can he be out of sight already?'

'He could have reached one of the farms, couldn't he?' said Emma.

'Perhaps ... but only if he moved very quickly,' said Peter. 'And when we left he was sitting down.'

'Maybe he opened a door in the stone and walked inside,' said Michael.

'There's one obvious place where he could easily be out of our sight,' said Peter, 'and that's halfway up the mountain, behind us.'

'He wouldn't follow us,' said Emma, taking a fistful of the sleeve of Peter's anorak and shaking his arm slightly. 'He wouldn't. Why would he follow us?'

'I don't know. To see what we're going to do, perhaps. I really can't see where else he could be.'

'Then let's hide,' said Emma.

'What's the point? He knows which way we're going, he's only got to follow the path. He can keep well below us and out of sight and still know exactly how far we've got by our voices. On a day like this, they'd carry well.'

'In that case,' said Michael, 'we leave the track at once and circle round to the spring – making a pact not to say a word so that he can't hear where we are.'

'Yes,' said Peter. 'Then we get lost and miss the spring and he follows us anyway. All right, we don't talk, but have you really listened to the din we make scrabbling up here and kicking stones? Do you think any of us is capable of going more quietly? And apart from the noise, as soon as we leave the track we blaze a trail that even *I* could follow. It's almost funny. Look!'

They looked down the track towards the last steep section, now just out of sight below a shallow outcrop of rock, and to the right of the rock they could see the scarred earth, and the crushed thistles, where they had scrambled in Michael's wake towards more level ground.

'What *do* you suggest?' said Michael.

'That we go on as we'd planned to do. If he is following

us we're not capable of losing him. Shall we have some lunch here where it's reasonably comfortable to sit down?'

'Having just suggested that a reasonably hostile man is probably creeping up the mountain behind us, how can you say let's sit about and eat?' said Michael. 'Who on earth is he? How did he *know* everything? Aren't you curious?'

'I don't know who he is – and we're no less safe here than we would be higher up.'

'Shouldn't we try and work out who he is?'

'How could we possibly do that? We just keep going. There's nothing else we can do.'

'Well. It *is* nearly one,' said Michael.

Peter took off his anorak and spread it on the ground below the rock face. He sat on it and Michael crouched uncomfortably beside him. They both waited for Emma to unpack the picnic.

'Do I have to get everything out?' she said.

'What's the matter?' said Peter. 'Do you want to be ready for a quick getaway?'

'Just get out the coffee and the first packet of sandwiches,' said Michael.

'Have you both lost your appetites?' said Peter.

Emma poured the coffee and opened a beautifully wrapped packet of cheese-and-tomato sandwiches. She sat down beside Peter with her back to the rock. From a sitting position the edge of the plateau looked quite sharp, as though the ground dropped sheer away from it, although they knew perfectly well that it in fact sloped quite gradually.

'I keep expecting his head to appear over the edge there,' said Emma.

'With a hand on either side,' said Michael. 'I know. So do I.'

'He wouldn't appear like that anyway,' said Peter, with

his mouth full. 'You'd see him walking upright towards you – it's not that steep, we've just walked up it you know.'

'I'm not at *all* hungry,' said Emma.

'Eat something,' said Peter.

'I've got butterflies.'

'Well, feed them. Here,' he rummaged in the rucksack, 'send down a banana, that'll give them something to think about.'

'He's cock-a-hoop,' said Michael, 'because I've been proved wrong – the whole thing *is* a bit weird after all. It's what he thought it was, and he's gloating.'

'It can't be what I thought it was, because I didn't know *what* it was.'

'Well, why are you so calm and cheerful?' said Michael.

'Because I wanted to come up here and I'm up here. I don't know why you worry. If he *is* following us he's going to keep out of sight to see what we do, so why bother about him?'

'Suppose we find the spring and he decides to come *in* sight and bother about *us*? What then?'

'Wait and see,' said Peter, selecting another sandwich. 'Do have something to eat to keep your strength up.'

'And what about Emma?' said Michael. 'Aren't we supposed to be looking after her? She's scared and I'm not surprised. Perhaps we ought to take her home again.'

'Nonsense!' said Peter. 'Mrs Myer said the calmer Emma looked, the more scared she really was. She's ashen and rigid now, which obviously means she's really extremely composed and confident.'

Emma laughed politely. 'There are an awful lot of things crawling about on this rock,' she said, by way of changing the subject.

'That's right,' said Peter. 'It's their home.'

'Oh, you're a real nature boy, aren't you?' said Michael. 'Must be pretty wild country up in Leeds.'

'We do have moors up there, you know. The Industrial North doesn't stretch from coast to coast.'

Emma leaned forward to take a sandwich and at that moment the sun went in. 'Oh no,' she said, 'it'll be chilly sitting here if there's no sun.'

'It's only a small cloud,' said Peter, squinting up at it. 'Anyway, we'll be moving on in a minute.'

'Huh!' said Michael in surprise, as a large single drop of rain fell on the back of his hand.

'I don't believe it,' said Emma. 'Out of a clear blue sky.'

'No, out of a small black cloud,' said Peter. 'It can only be a shower.'

Two or three more drops fell, loudly, against the rock.

'Do you suppose we ought to look for shelter?' said Michael.

Drops began to fall regularly, though they were still very widely spaced.

'Must be a thundershower with these huge drops,' said Peter. The sun had still not reappeared from behind its cloud and the air was grey. They shivered. Michael drained his coffee mug.

'If everyone's had enough, shall we clear up and find a rock to get behind?' he said.

Emma held out the snake glasses. 'Put them in, please,' she said. 'I don't want to carry them.'

The rain began to fall steadily and the sky darkened a little more. 'A real thundershower,' said Peter, a little uneasily, helping to put things away.

Michael picked up the rucksack and turned up the collar of his donkey-jacket. He crossed to the left of the rock wall, from where it was possible to see that the plateau was enclosed by long arms of earth- and grass-covered rock which sloped gently down to their feet and offered a fairly easy route up. As he began to climb, he saw that already little rivulets of water were trickling down towards him. And as he reached the top of the climb, with the others at his heels, the rain was beating down steadily and the sky was so dark that they had difficulty in seeing far ahead. Way off to their left, away from the track – which was to the right of where they stood – a pile of large rocks from some long-past avalanche seemed to offer hope of shelter. Instinctively Michael began to run towards them.

'Don't go too far off course,' Peter yelled after him.

'I don't want to get soaked,' Michael called, still running.

'I'd rather get soaked than lost,' said Peter, who had hold of Emma's sleeve and was dragging her along, half-blinded by the beating rain, in his wake.

There was no cave or inlet of any kind in the rocks when they reached them. They afforded no more shelter than the open plateau had.

'We're so wet already, does it matter?' said Peter.

'Come on,' said Michael, who had seen a huge sloping outcrop of rock quite a way beyond. 'That'll do.'

Peter looked behind him. Sheets of grey rain limited his field of vision to a few feet. It was, if anything, slightly darker than before. 'Don't go farther!' he called to Michael's receding figure. 'Suppose it stays like this for the rest of the day – we'll never find the path down.'

Emma pulled free of Peter and ran after Michael, her head down as if she thought she could keep the rain off that way – apparently not realizing that she was already soaked almost to the skin.

Peter sank down by the first pile of rocks: from there he could just make out the big outcrop and the two figures that sought its minimal shelter, and he also thought he could remember the route back to the track. 'I'll stay here,' he called to them. 'Then we won't get lost.'

Michael's voice called back, but the rain beat and hissed on the rocks and the dry ground drank it loudly and all that Peter heard were some words about a freak storm.

Rain poured down all over him, loudly, relentlessly, and streamed over the rock he leant on and ran down his neck. It was cold. He tried to look up at the sky for some sign of a break, but the beating rain forced him to close his eyes. He knew nothing about the weather in this part of the country but he couldn't believe that this was going to abate for hours. He began to wonder if they ought to try to make their way down at once. The narrow track would be streaming with water by now, and slippery with mud, but it would get worse and then night would come and it would be dark.

Then with a shock he realized that it was already totally dark, as dark as any night could be. He kept trying to think what was the sensible thing to do, and because the rain was too loud for him to think properly he whispered to himself. 'If we start sliding about now in the dark and the rain, we may get lost and we may break our necks,' he said, 'but every minute we wait here the track gets wetter and less passable.' Then he remembered Mrs White's assurance that the weather would be fine, and how he wouldn't have believed anybody if they had told him, five or even two minutes before the first drop of rain, that there was going to be a storm like this; and he thought that Michael was probably right – it was a freak storm that would end as suddenly as it had begun. It was just a question of enduring.

To take his mind off his own discomfort he pictured the Myers looking anxiously out of their windows. He wondered if the whole valley was being drenched or if it was just that a big cloud was sitting on top of the mountain.

Either way, the Myers were sure to have noticed. He wondered how Mrs White felt about her weather forecast now. Then he remembered the man at the stone and all the eyes he had sensed on them on their way up. Nothing could be watching them now, that was one thing, all eyes would be screwed up against the rain.

Somewhere out of sight above him a waterfall, or perhaps a new stream, seemed to be forming. At any rate, above the regular hiss of rain on rock and ground he could hear a murmuring that was new.

He struggled to read the time on his watch, which was luminous, but it became heavily rain-smeared as soon as he brought it out from under his cuff. Eventually he made out that it said ten past one – and that it had stopped. No amount of winding or shaking would start it again. It was supposed to be waterproof and he was annoyed.

The murmuring from the new waterfall was a musical sound and less monotonous than the rain's other noises because it rose and fell, almost like a chant. It was at once soothing and compelling. He caught himself listening for words in it.

The sky was no lighter, but he was suddenly sure that the rain was less heavy – he was aware of the separateness of the drops whereas earlier they had seemed to fall in one solid sheet. He squelched uncomfortably to his feet and peered about him. It was incredibly and amazingly dark. He had never been up a mountain in a storm before but he couldn't believe that this darkness, such a short time after noon, could be normal. He was suddenly seriously frightened. He thought he might join the others, even at the risk of losing the way back to the track. He looked up into the darkness where the peaceful chanting water was hidden, and then he thought that perhaps, instead of joining the others, he would move a little bit closer to that. It was a comforting noise and he was sure it was quite near. If he climbed straight up the pile of rocks he was on, he would find it, and then all he had to do was climb straight down again to be where he was now. He didn't see how he could get lost.

It wasn't easy to climb the wet rock with his slimy wet shoes and wet, slippery hands, but he managed, moving slowly, on all fours, and the singing called him on. When he reached the top of the rock pile the sound was quite loud, and peering forward into the darkness he made out one rock, not many feet ahead of him, that was slightly taller than the rest; he thought that the rain must have formed some kind of channel around it because this was where the sound came from. Unsure of his balance in the dark, he continued towards it on his hands and feet, crawling awkwardly like a badly made insect, and he wondered how running water could sound so like words; and then he wasn't sure if what he saw was a rock at all, or if it was a man sitting upright, just above him, making a beautiful chant that blended in the dark with every other liquid sound around him.

He crept a little nearer, not afraid, cautious only in case he should slip and fall back down again; and he saw through the lessening rain and the dark that it was a rock and it was a man, it was a rock in the shape of a seated man, it was a man made of grey rock and water – because the water that flowed down the figure and circled at its feet was part of it, rock and rain together making a man who was not quite human, a Rainrock whose mouth moved slowly as the beautiful chanted words came gently from him.

ON his knees, he listened to the Rainrock as it sang and he heard the words in its slow melodic chant. It sang about a woman in the valley who was crying because she was alone. It sang about a man who was laughing because he had just realized he was alive and free and was happy about it. It sang about sad things, like the child in a house close by the harbour wall who was ill and in pain, and funny things, like the three children on the mountain who thought they could shelter from this rain. It sang about a tree that was very old and dying; about some seedlings, newly planted out, which were facing the ordeal of their first night in the wild world; about a fish trapped in a pool, waiting for the rains to raise the level of the river and release it again; about a small beetle on its back below a rock a few feet away, constantly assailed by drips of water from above and unable to right itself; and even about the shifting by the wind of some topsoil from one field to another.

It sang of everything that moved, or lived, or existed, of all reality, and Peter held on to the ground beneath him, knowing that the world was whole and that it was turning; he was suddenly aware of the depth of cold, warm, living, populated earth under his body, right down to the roots of the mountain and far, far below it. He knew that, hemmed in as he was by darkness and rain, and blunted as his senses were by these, the world had not after all shrunk to the few feet he was physically aware of, but was there, all there, alive and functioning, above and below ground, all the time.

Gradually the rain ceased, and the sky cleared, although it was still totally dark. Stars shone. And still the Rainrock sang the events of the valley to the starry night sky.

Below him Peter heard the voices of the others and he knew that they had left their inadequate shelter and were looking for him. He knew it not only because he could hear them but because the Rainrock, its voice fading now, included their movements in its chant.

Gradually, as no more fell from the sky, the water that had run noisily down the mountain and among the rocks was absorbed into the earth. And as its sound died down, so the voice of the Rainrock dimmed and its figure faded. Peter, staring by starlight at the smaller, rounder rocks where he had seen its form, wondered for a moment if it had not, after all, been an illusion. At the same time he knew instinctively that an illusion would have blunted his perception of the real world, not sharpened it until it could encompass the whole valley and even the other side of the mountain.

He watched as Michael and Emma made their way slowly

up to his level, and, still under the influence of the chant, he wondered if their approach was any more significant than the tunnelling under the valley floor of hundreds of worms or the struggles of the small beetle. While the others climbed on up, Peter moved to where the beetle was, found it in the circumstances described by the Rainrock, and turned it on to its feet with his forefinger. It hurried into a crevice and Peter wondered if the Rainrock, invisible and inaudible as it might be now, relayed to the stars this change of fortune in the beetle's life.

'Was that weird voice coming from here?' said Michael. His clothes were saturated and creased and most of his self-assurance gone. He and Emma were hand in hand. Peter thought of the babes in the wood.

'You heard it?' he said.

'At first we thought it was just the noise of the water, but then it got louder and we were sure there were words. It's gone now,' he added unnecessarily. They listened meekly while Peter told them everything that he had heard. 'Who'd have thought we'd been up here so long?' said Michael.

'I don't feel as if it *has* been very long,' said Peter, 'I'm not hungry again, and I was only just beginning to get cramp when the song ended.'

'It must have been long if it sang all that,' said Michael sadly. 'But I can't tell. My watch has stopped, has yours? And Emma looked at the compass just now and the needle just swings round loosely and points anywhere. It must have been some kind of electrical storm. Would that do it?'

'I think it's only been about half an hour,' said Peter.

'No. It's night.'

'Yes, but not tonight. I mean it's not the night of this day. The moon was almost full last night. There's no moon at all now, though the sky is clear.'

Michael looked at him for a moment without speaking. Then he said, 'We've been talking. We want to go down straight away.'

'No, we must go on – now,' said Peter.

'It's dark. We must go down, we must get back.'

'We can't go back now,' said Peter patiently. 'Something has changed and we don't know how much. If we go down there now, we may never get back to where we were. We have to go on, we have to do the round trip.' He turned away from them and began to move on upwards, bearing right in the hope of hitting on the track.

Emma pulled her hand away from Michael and called after Peter. 'I want to go home!' she said, and as soon as Peter turned to look at her she began to make her way down the rocky path, to demonstrate.

'That isn't the way home,' Peter shouted at her. 'Don't you understand? *This* is the way home,' and he went on up, ignoring them both.

Michael, looking from one to the other, saw Emma's panic-stricken and perilous descent and the assurance with which Peter made his way steadily upwards.

'We must go with him,' he called down to Emma.

She stopped. 'You agreed!' she said.

'We must keep together,' said Michael, almost pleadingly.

'Then let him come with us,' said Emma. 'If we both go down, he'll come too.'

'No, he's going up,' said Michael. 'We're better off together.'

'Well, you and I will be together. And as soon as we get down we'll tell them and they'll send a search-party up for Peter. *Please!*'

'I'd rather be with him,' said Michael sheepishly. 'He understands it better than we do.'

When she saw that he really wasn't going to come with

her, there was one moment when Emma considered going back alone. Then she climbed slowly up to Michael, and past him, and on up after Peter. Michael followed.

'All I can think of is that I want to be safe,' she said. 'I'd leave you both up here, lost, if I thought I dared go down by myself.'

'I'm only going with him because I think I'll be safer,' said Michael.

'We're not very noble, are we?'

'Not very.'

'We've been talking,' said Michael again, when his voice could reach Peter, 'and we think the man at the stone is the man in the little watercolour – only older.'

'Perhaps,' said Peter.

'Well, who *is* he?' said Michael. 'If she says she painted him when she was about your age, that would make him more than ten years older than her now, even older than the tramp – but he wasn't.'

'No,' said Peter, picking his way carefully upwards. 'We've struck the path again now, do you see?'

'Look, why won't we talk about him? We must work out who he is,' said Michael.

'I don't see how we can.'

The track was noticeably steeper now, and they had to use their hands to help them almost all the time.

'But how did he know ... everything ...'

'Don't go on about it. It doesn't matter. Everything we do is known – even the number of ants we've accidentally squashed on the way up, I expect.' Peter stopped, out of breath, and the other two behind him. 'I think that really is the top of the mountain,' he said. 'I think that really is it at last. Do you want me to take the rucksack for a bit?'

'I left it,' said Michael.

'What!'

'I left it where we sheltered. Emma and I didn't mean to come on up, we were only coming to fetch you down again. Does it matter? It's much easier without it.'

'All right, we'll pick it up on our way down again.'

'I'm sorry,' said Michael.

'All right,' said Peter, who was faintly embarrassed by the new deference.

While they climbed they had concentrated solely on the ground they were covering. Now that they had paused for breath they looked around, at the dark rocks beside them, at the lights of the village and the boats in the harbour so small below, and at the sky which they seemed to be approaching.

'It's those stars!' said Michael suddenly. 'Look! Peter!'

'I know,' said Peter, beginning to climb again.

'What stars?' said Emma.

They climbed perhaps twenty feet in silence and then Peter stopped again and stood looking upwards. 'Look at them again,' he said. 'Don't you see anything unusual about them?'

Michael let out a long sigh. In a sky full of stars, one patch was different to the rest. The constellation of Aquarius, low on the mountain top, was composed not of stars made small by distance but of small lights, quite close to – lights in the windows of a dark castle.

12 THEY stood still, slightly breathless and leaning forward to compensate for the slope of the path.

'It *is* a castle,' said Emma, 'but unless you look carefully it just blends into the black sky.'

'What do we do about it?' said Michael flatly. The night was now somewhat less cold, and their clothes were beginning to dry, which somehow made them look even worse than they had when they were wet.

Peter was already walking and climbing upwards. Michael followed. So did Emma, but she said, 'Hadn't we better decide what we're going to do?'

'We can't know till we get there,' said Peter.

They had to move very slowly because the wet ground was treacherous and any attempt at speed sent drops of mud flicking high into the air.

'But do we want to get to it?' said Emma, almost tear-fully, though she continued to follow. 'Suppose it's danger-ous?'

Peter paused for a rest, leaning forward against the moun-tain and embracing a rock with both arms. It's . . .' he said, and looked upwards. Emma remembered the first evening and the way Peter had gazed up at the mountain from the lane, with less understanding than now but with the same sort of expression on his face. 'It's inevitable,' he said eventually and, that settled, continued to make his way upwards, mostly by the path but occasionally zigzagging to avoid the vertical parts which the rain had turned into slides.

And they drew nearer until there was no question that it was a castle – a small castle, planted heavily on this, the highest point of the mountain. It had walls built of big slabs of weatherworn local stone, crenellated battlements and an enormous oak door set deep in an arch to the far right. What they had taken to be the bottom two stars in the constellation of Aquarius were in fact two lanterns which were suspended from old iron hooks at each side of the archway, high up and well out of reach. Small, square openings, quite unlike the arrow slits one might have ex-pected, appeared in the towering walls at uneven intervals, each containing a lantern and forming part of the Aquarius pattern. The lanterns hung steady, the flames did not flicker, there was no movement at all. The patchy light revealed that tall grass covered the castle's roots and pushed up through cracks in the paving under the arch which held the door. Apart from that there was no evidence that the castle was in any way ruined, and, equally, apart from the imperturbable lanterns, no sign of habitation. It gave the children a curious feeling, as they stood a few feet back and looked at it, because it was so obviously remote, abandoned and empty, and yet at the same time so obviously alive and cared for.

'Shall I knock on the door?' said Peter. It was quite obvious that he was sure someone was going to knock and wondered only which of them it was to be.

Michael looked startled. 'No!' he said.

'Why not?'

Michael smiled rather forlornly. 'Someone might open it,' he said. 'I can't face any more today.'

'But we have to face it,' said Peter. 'It's here and we can't go back.'

'We don't have to go in, though.'

'Then what do you suggest? That we sit on the grass and wait?'

'It isn't always here,' said Michael. 'It isn't always this night. Things are bound to get back to normal?'

'They can't,' said Peter patiently. 'Time is suspended. We could sit here for what would seem like years and nothing would change. Something is happening and it's only half-way through. I told you. Unless we allow it to finish we'll never get back to the point where we were – to the day when we started off to walk up here. We don't have a choice. We can only postpone the inevitable, and there's no point in that is there?'

'How do you *know* all this?'

'I don't know it the way you mean. I just feel it.'

'We're playing with things we don't understand,' said Michael.

'Of *course* we are. But we burned our boats back at the standing stone. Didn't you know that? He told us we couldn't go on someone else's Quest. That means we've made it ours. You were keen enough to go on then – you were the one he tried to hold, because he knew you were the leader – then. You can't back out now. Do you understand? I don't mean you mustn't, I mean you bloody *can't*.'

They stared at each other, from their reversed positions, and Emma said softly, 'I have an Uncle who says if you have to do something it's better to get it over and done with.'

The tension broke as both boys began to laugh. 'Oh Emma,' said Michael, the look of strain gone from his face. 'How many Uncles have you got?'

Emma blushed.

'One?' said Peter, putting his arm round her.

Emma stared solidly back at him.

'None!' said Michael. 'Emma, you haven't got any Uncles, have you? Not a one!'

Emma investigated a grazed knuckle very closely.

Peter rocked her slightly. 'It doesn't matter,' he said. 'You know that, don't you? It works.'

'Long live Emma's Uncles,' said Michael. 'And we may as well take the advice of that last one and get on with it.'

Peter glanced down the mountain, at the lights of the village, and then back at the castle, framed in a dark sky full of genuine stars. Then he walked in under the archway to the great door. Michael followed, saying, 'It's really only a keep,' as if he wanted to diminish it before he got too close. Emma stayed just outside the deep arch, under one of the lamps.

Inside the arch it was colder and there was no bell-pull or door knocker. Indeed the door was quite unadorned apart from a massive keyhole, in which there was no key. Peter banged with his fist, and the solid oak swallowed the sound. Though it was so slight, the noise made Emma feel exposed and she moved into the porch with the others.

The silence began to hang heavily, and nothing changed; no sound of movement came from within the castle. The patches of light thrown on the ground by the lanterns remained steady. Peter raised both fists and banged three times, with all his strength. This time the sound seemed to find its way farther into the interior. Automatically, they stepped back a little — and waited. Moments of time passed by and nothing happened, no sound from within or without the castle, no breath of wind, as if they were in limbo. Nothing — except a growing sense of expectancy, which they all picked up and which made them uneasy.

Michael signed silently to Peter, who nodded, and at exactly the same moment he and Peter thudded both their fists against the wood, twice. They waited and Peter rubbed the back of his bruised hands on the seat of his wet trousers, to cool them.

Nothing.

Peter turned away from the door and looked out over the mountain. 'I was so sure we were meant to get in,' he said.

Michael was examining the door very carefully. 'It must be a massive lock to have a keyhole this size,' he said. He began to search the porch methodically, picking with his fingertips at the broken stones of the floor and running his hands over the walls as high as he could reach. But there were no loose stones, no crevices or niches, no obvious place where a large key might lie hidden. He worked his way steadily towards the porch entrance. He looked up at the lanterns, far above their heads. Then he bent slightly and made a cup of his hands, and Peter, with resignation, allowed himself to be given a leg up. Head level with the left-hand lantern and splayed hands clawing at the rough wall, he croaked, 'No,' and was allowed to descend. They paused a moment and then made the same assault on the right-hand lantern, Peter peering well down into the base where the melted wax lay. But no key was hidden there, and in fact there was barely room in the lanterns for a key of a size to move the great lock.

Michael brushed his hands together. Peter seemed almost at a loss; then he said, 'So let's walk round it and see if there's another way in.' He whispered, and he wasn't sure why, unless it was because the sense of expectancy which hung in the air was so strong that it seemed almost like a presence. And it was undoubtedly emanating from the castle, which waited, in a breathless frozen moment, so untouched by passing time that even when Peter, panting with the effort, had brought his head up level with the flames in the lanterns, they did not move or flicker by a millimetre.

Staying very close together, they left the arch behind them and moved slowly along with the castle wall on their right. They tried to move quietly, but the lanterns were more effective as beacon lights than as street lamps, and though the ground was almost level they stumbled on the odd stone with a clatter that broke the silence and seemed quite out of place.

'This wall's longer than I thought,' said Peter. He sounded abstracted. From the moment he had first seen the castle, he had lived in imagination through an enormous variety of dangers and difficulties – but not this one. Trouble, he had thought, would come when they saw what was inside; being locked out was not a possibility he had considered.

An urgent hand clutched his elbow, and Emma hissed, 'Look behind us!'

He looked back. After about three minutes of steady walking, the archway which held the door was still no more than two feet behind them. They stood very still, very close, and stared.

'Come on!' said Peter sharply, and turning from the arch he went on the way they had been going, moving far more quickly than before, stumbling, with the others tight up to his heels. When they were breathless with exertion, and their efforts should have taken them completely round the castle, Peter thought he might risk a glance behind them, but Emma had not been able to wait. 'It's following us,' she whispered miserably. Not two feet behind them was the dark arch, whose two lamps burned steadily, and ahead of them stretched the wall of the keep, just as it had before they had started.

'The castle is turning,' said Peter softly, as if he was dredging the idea up from the very bottom of his mind. 'I half remember something – no, I think I forget it – but it's turning – we are here – this is our place – we can't go anywhere else. It must be the door.'

They had no difficulty in walking the three steps back to the mouth of the arch.

'It wants us inside,' said Emma. 'Why does it keep us out? What are we supposed to do?'

'Something!' said Peter. 'It's waiting for us to do something. Can't you feel it?'

'There's a keyhole, but no key,' said Michael. 'We've looked everywhere where a key could possibly be hidden. Nothing happens when we knock. We couldn't pick that lock with anything less than a crowbar. There is no possible way we could break down that door.'

Peter chewed his finger and leant unhappily against the arch. Michael, suddenly very tired, sat down on the ground, electing, after a few nasty seconds when he wasn't sure where he could turn his back with safety, to face the porch. Emma stood between them staring at the beautiful old door.

'Oh, *please* let us in,' she said.

And the door swung quietly and immediately open, inwards, on to a dark passage.

13 'WHY didn't we bring a torch?' said Michael.

'If we're really going in,' said Emma, 'do you suppose it would matter if we took one of the lanterns with us?'

'Is that your Uncle talking, or you?' said Michael.

'I think it's only me.'

'Shall we?' Michael asked Peter.

Peter looked doubtful. 'They belong there, rather, don't they?' he said.

'It's completely dark inside,' said Michael. 'We don't know what we'd walk into.'

The door stood back, at right angles to its frame, waiting for them, and Michael helped Peter up the wall again.

No matter how hard he tried, and no matter how much either brute force or intelligence he applied, Peter could not even make the lantern move, let alone unhook it from its place. Dazzled by the steady candle-flame, he found it almost impossible to see how the lantern was fixed to its hook. Because Michael was naturally convinced he could do better, Peter bent double and allowed his back to be used as a ladder. But the lantern remained where it was, unaffected by Michael's efforts.

'I don't suppose anyone's got a box of matches?' said Michael hopefully, when he was on the ground again.

'We'll join hands and go in single file,' said Peter, 'with Emma in the middle.'

'Who goes first?' said Michael.

'I will.'

The light from the porch lanterns extended a very short way beyond the open door, and they could see that a passage ran straight ahead – which was odd because the bulk of the keep was to the left of the door, and yet the passage seemed to run just inside the right-hand outside wall.

It was even harder to go through the door than it had been to knock on it; but once they were well inside, and no sound or movement greeted their approach, they found it possible to move along the passage until, with a thick and heavy sound – not loud but somehow very final – the oak door closed behind them, cutting off the light completely.

Emma clawed at Peter's hand so roughly that he grunted, and then she tried to pull back the way they had come. Michael tried to stand quite still and listen, and Peter tried to keep up the forward movement; so that for a moment they struggled in total confusion and didn't move in either direction.

'Listen,' Peter whispered, 'you only want to get out again now that you can't. When you could, you were prepared to come on with me.'

Wedged between them and unable to free her hands, Emma stood quietly, shivering. Peter allowed them to stand for a moment and listen to the silence. He half hoped his eyes would accustom themselves to the dark and half realized that they would not. He stared at the million coloured sparks that make up darkness and then said to Emma, 'Hold on to the back of my windcheater. I want both hands.'

They let him lead them on again.

Peter walked along the stone floor, whose coldness was just beginning to seep through the soles of his shoes, with his right hand sliding along the rough stone wall and his left hand straight out in front of him. This bit he didn't like at all and he wished it would hurry up and resolve itself into the next stage, whatever that was. The roughness of the right-hand wall under his hand set his teeth on edge – yet he had to keep contact with it in case they came to a corner. The fingers of his left hand curled in apprehension at what they might touch, and it was only the knowledge that if his hand didn't travel ahead he might walk face-first into something that enabled him to keep his arm out.

The stone gave off coldness on all sides. Peter could hear Emma's teeth chattering faintly behind him, and his own jaw ached with clenching. He had a sudden unreasoning fear that for all his precautions with both hands he might walk straight into a pit in the flagged floor. He took to sliding his feet forward instead of picking them up with each step, so that he would have some warning of any opening in the ground.

Just when his mind was concentrated fully on his feet, and the dread possibility of a fall deep into cold darkness, the fingertips of his left hand touched stone.

'Stop,' he whispered, and he meant it to sound calm, but it didn't because his jaw was stiff with cold and fear. 'I think the passage turns left,' he added quickly, in case they thought he had met something terrible. With his right hand, he felt the corner of the wall and then, stretching his left arm out and back, his fingers found the sharp corner on that side, too. 'Yes, it turns left,' he said, and turned left with it.

The new section of passage was exactly like the first. There was no glimmer of light, and the floor and walls were plain, rough, cold stone. Though it was not at all stuffy, there was no indication of any openings and he began to wonder about air. His feet scuffed slowly along the ground and it occurred to him how terrifyingly sinister his approach would sound to anyone up ahead. He realized that he could quite easily frighten himself with the sound of his own footsteps.

Then he wondered how high the passage was, and for some reason his scalp crawled. He told himself that the funny little procession he was leading was quite inevitable, but the idea didn't comfort him, although he believed it. He wondered what the others thought about it. Did they believe that something inevitable must be 'good' in the end? But if there was no clear-cut right or wrong in this Quest, there was no clear-cut good or evil, either. 'Michael says I understand it better than they do,' he thought, 'but all I understand is that I don't understand.'

At that moment his outstretched left hand touched stone again and he stopped.

'Another corner?' came Michael's voice from behind.

'Yes.'

'Which way?'

'Left.'

'Left again?' hissed Michael hoarsely. 'But if we go along there, we'll be covering the third side of a square!'

'I wish you'd use your normal voice,' said Peter irritably. 'You give me the creeps.'

'Won't we?' Michael persisted.

'There's no other way,' said Peter, when he had explored cautiously with both hands to make sure.

He led them left.

'Do you think this passage leads right round the castle, just inside the wall?' said Michael. 'Each stretch seems about the same length.'

Peter didn't answer. He wanted to listen and not talk. Surely the farther they went, the nearer they must be to wherever they were going? Or did things not necessarily work that way? The thought confused him and he tried to go on without thinking. He wished that it had occurred to him to count his steps along the first two sections of passage so that he could check if this one was indeed the same length. He felt damp and cold and physically uncomfortable. He found he was becoming unreasonably irritated by the weight of Emma's clutching hands on the back of his anorak. All sense of suspense was gone. He was as nearly bored as a lingering fear would allow. Then his outstretched fingers found stone again, and again the passage turned left.

'That's the *fourth* side of a square,' Michael carped from behind him.

'There's no other way,' said Peter. 'What else can I do? Do you want to go back?'

'No point,' said Michael. 'This last stretch'll lead us back to the door where we started.'

'Stop,' said Peter, as he rounded the corner. 'There's a light ahead.' They stopped and stood close together, Peter flat against the right-hand wall so that the other two could see past him.

It was a diffused rather than a particular light and it revealed nothing very much because it was so faint. It was just that at the far end of this stretch of the passage it was not quite dark.

'There you are,' said Michael. 'That'll be the door, down at the end there, and the light comes from the lamps outside.'

'You think the door's open again?' said Peter.

'The wind shut it,' said Michael. 'The wind's opened it again.'

It was several seconds before Peter began to walk again, but when he did he moved at the same speed as before, with no apparent apprehension. When they were halfway between the corner and the dim glow, he said, 'If the light was from the open door it would come from the right, not from the left.' A few paces on and they could see that there was a blank wall ahead of them, and that the right-hand wall was unbroken by any passage entrance. But there was an opening in the left-hand wall, at the far end, and it was from this that the weak light came.

'We're not walking round the outside,' said Peter, with a curious excitement in his voice, 'we're spiralling in towards the centre.'

John Husford

14 HE turned left, where he had to, and he was glad of his determination not to transmit fear to Emma because this enabled him to turn the corner at a steady pace, although his stomach muscles had formed a tight knot of apprehension. The passageway that was revealed when he was round the corner looked exactly as he imagined the previous stretches had looked: a flagged stone floor, rough walls made of great blocks cut from what looked like local rock, and a high ceiling lost in shadows; and at the end a blank wall, and to the left of it an opening through which a brighter light shone out – just about what he might have expected, and yet there was something odd that he couldn't place.

He paused to look back. Michael, who had been quite convinced that they would find themselves anticlimactically outside the castle, was sullen. Emma had reached that point in fear, Peter saw, where she would follow whoever led.

Peter went on, a funny sort of exhilaration in him. He had to suppress a tendency to go too fast rather than to hang back.

None of them spoke and Peter tried to work out in his mind what it was that was strange. It was an unobvious strangeness – like the strangeness when a clock stops ticking or a fridge stops humming and you don't at first realize what it is that's different, missing.

Something was missing.

Cobwebs.

There were no cobwebs, there was no moss or lichen or fungus of any sort; there were no dips in the flagstones of the kind worn by many feet; the pits and crevices in the walls were there because of the composition of the stone, not because of the ravages of time. The castle wasn't old, could hardly be new, must therefore exist quite outside time.

For company, he conveyed this idea to Michael, which was a mistake because Michael immediately began to think about it. 'But if it exists outside time and we're inside it, what could that do to us?' he said. 'And when we get out where will we be? We shouldn't have come in. Do you think we ought to go on?'

'Don't think about it,' said Peter wearily, 'just do it.' And, talking, he turned the next left corner into a lightness that was brighter than any they had seen before. He stopped sharply because this was obviously the centre of the castle.

The three of them huddled damply in the archway where they found themselves and looked on to an enormous courtyard, open to the starry sky above but brightly lit by hundreds, literally hundreds, of lamps that hung all over the four stone walls. The courtyard was not paved and the grassy floor was uneven and scattered with stones, as if the outer walls and passages had just been dumped down on the flat top of the mountain. There was nobody in sight, and all was quiet except for the soft swish of water.

In the centre of the courtyard stood a small tree, barely more than a tall shrub, and it curved its puny branches protectively over a large rock. This rock looked, even from a distance, somewhat different to the rocks they had passed on the way up the mountain, and it had a deep horizontal cleft in it, like a huge mouth with a projecting lower lip, and the soft watery sounds seemed to come from inside.

However hard they looked, straining their eyes into the far corners of the great enclosure, they could see nothing else, and no person or thing appeared to watch their approach.

They waited, quite still, but nothing changed, nothing moved. Michael let out a long sigh and laughed with relief. Even Emma perked up. And when Peter began to move towards the tree and the rock, Emma let go of his anorak and Michael of her hand and they went with him quite willingly.

'Do you see the rock?' said Michael. 'It's the same stuff as Mrs White's stone – and the stone with the float on it.'

'I know,' said Peter. He paused just short of the rock. 'Don't you feel exposed here?' he said.

That stopped them, and all three examined the four surrounding walls, with their dozens upon dozens of gleaming lanterns. But there were no windows or apertures in these walls, no head looked over the battlements, no figure stood in the arch through which they had come, no one waited in the courtyard itself. They relaxed, and went on.

The strange, dark, quartz-like rock was about as high as Michael and within its mouth, gurgling faintly, a clear spring bubbled, whose waters flowed over the lower lip and then disappeared into a small fissure in the earth below.

They stood in a row and admired it. Even if they had not seen Mrs White's painting of it, each one felt sure it would have been obvious that this was 'her' spring.

Emma's face had regained some of its pinkness. 'Come on,' she said eagerly, and she leant forward and reached out her hands to cup some of the water.

But, 'Don't drink from the spring,' said a calm voice behind them.

Although fifty or sixty years must have passed since Mrs White painted him, he hadn't aged at all. And when, instead of looking at an inept watercolour, they looked at the man himself – young and dark, bearded and golden-eyed – they knew that he was the man at the stone, and that he had travelled back through many years to warn them, in the guise of the tramp, not to go mountaineering. They stood in a row with their back to the spring and felt no fear at all.

'It was not your Quest,' he said.

'She wanted us to come,' said Peter.

'Of course. What were you going to do?'

'Divert the spring into the main water-supply for the village.'

'Why?'

'Because she believed it was magic – and that everybody should share it.'

Somehow it seemed that the lanterns illuminated them far more than they illuminated the man, which was slightly embarrassing. Also, he was so pleasant and so dignified, dressed in his dark, monkish robes, that they felt, not frightened, not endangered, but awkward. They had been caught trespassing, and however well the landowner took it, the fact remained that they shouldn't have been there.

'It is not,' he said, 'up to you to decide such matters.' Then he smiled. 'The spring water is administered most carefully,' he said. 'Some of it indeed finds it way into

Mrs White's well, and you may tell her so. But it's strong medicine, too strong for most.'

'How do you stop the tourists coming up here?' said Michael.

'They come. The spring is not easy to find and it is usually missed. Of those few who find it, fewer drink. And of those who drink there may be one in ten years, like Mrs White, who gains. The rest go home talking about sunstroke and exposure. Mr Myer, for instance, has an instinctive dislike of the whole mountain. He doesn't know why. But it is simply because certain people will always feel uneasy when they sense the presence of a deeper knowledge. It's a natural reaction, and protective, because people's needs, and their purposes, differ. It's very important that you realize this because don't think, for one moment, that Mr Myer is inferior because this is not for him, nor that you are inferior, because it is not for you – not yet.'

'So you tried to stop *us*,' said Peter, 'because you knew why we were coming? Were the starlings watching us?'

'Starlings have great curiosity,' said the man. 'They may have been watching you.'

'Peter thought the starlings were spying on us and reporting back to someone,' said Emma chattily. If this man owned the mountain, she thought, she would feel safe on any part of it in any kind of darkness or storm.

'Once you select a hypothesis it is easy to make everything fit it,' said the man. 'Starlings are ubiquitous. I don't need spies. The earth knows what's happening.'

'Do you mean the Rainrock with his song?' said Peter.

'Some people see it that way.'

'You shouldn't have told us not to play that game with the glass,' said Michael. 'It told Peter not to go.'

'Did it?' He laughed. 'I was sure your wishful thinking would have it spelling out promises of treasure and good fortune up here.' He looked at each of them, smiling, and then said, 'Don't be offended, but you must go home very soon.'

'Is this where you live?' said Emma. 'Can't we stay here for a bit with you?'

'Very soon I shall go and things will change. Then you must go down the mountain.'

He turned slightly away, as if he was going there and then, and Peter said urgently, 'Can I ask you something?'

The man turned back and waited. Apart from the spring, it was amazingly quiet on top of this mountain – no wind, no owls or nightjars, not even the distant bark of a dog from one of the farms below. Peter thought that he might be going to stammer, and tried to formulate a complete sentence so that it would sound sensible. If one wasn't meant to drink the spring water, it seemed to him quite possible that one wasn't meant to know certain things either, and he was afraid of overstepping the mark.

He said, 'I want to know about the rock,' and because the sentence came out neatly and unstumbled-upon, and because the man listened without frowning, everything came out: how he had seen Mrs White in the float, which was stuck to a piece of the rock, and what Mrs White had said, when she held her piece of rock – about the cold and the dark and the something that moved there – and how the spectacles made from the gold vein in the rock had revealed the auras around people.

The man watched Peter intently while he spoke and for a moment or two after he had finished. Then he said, 'The water widens perception, the gold deepens it and the rock itself has communicative powers. When Mrs White was young and drank the spring water, she saw all the possibilities just for a brief moment, and she took away with her a piece of the rock that had chipped off from the rest. And later she split it apart to remove the gold, and she had the glasses made and she understands their power and she uses them well. The rock she does not understand. She didn't use it to call you. She was thinking about you all, and had been ever since she knew you were coming, because she wanted you to visit her. And on that day, she wandered about holding the stone, wishing on it because she believes it may be a wishing stone, which it is not. And at one point she even looked down into the well. That was the moment when you, by chance, picked up the stone in the Myers' cottage. And she saw your face in the bottom of the well when you saw hers at the top. Do you understand?'

'No – why in the well?'

'The stone communicates visually when there is a suitable surface – a glass float, water, a mirror even. When there is not, it uses the surface of the imagination. When you were in Mrs White's house and she picked up her half of the stone, I was here, thinking back to the theft of that piece of stone when she moved through the cold and the dark and took it from its place; and on the surface of her imagination that image appeared.'

'So she knew what the stone was saying – though she said she didn't?'

'Probably not. My thought processes are not the same as hers. Did you understand, when I made my stars shine and then sat and looked at them, that that was what had happened – that that was what you saw in the glass float?'

'Was it all right that I asked you to explain?' said Peter.

'You'll only remember what you've understood,' said the man, and he turned away sharply and Emma called out to him, 'What's your name?' and he said, 'Aquarius', and he wasn't there any more and a tremendous wind had arisen somewhere in the valley and its approach was like some great creature rushing up the mountainside, and in the same moment that they heard it coming it hit them and knocked them all on to the ground. As they fell they saw the walls of the castle turning, turning around them, and none of them knew whether the walls were actually moving or whether the fall had made them dizzy, and the walls spun faster until it seemed as though their spinning was creating the great wind. They lay on the ground because as soon as they tried to get up, the wind buffeted them over again, and the walls spun faster still, until they were just a blur, and less than a blur ... and then the walls and the castle were there no longer and the wind was over and they picked themselves up on a flat mountain-top on a fine night, breathless and unsteady on their feet, and saw that the rock which concealed the spring was infinitely smaller than they had thought – no more than a foot high, and so unremarkable that you might search the mountain for hours and never find it.

'So we were meant to find it,' said Peter, brushing earth from his elbows.

'Do you think it would be all right to have a drink from it now?' said Michael.

'He said not,' said Emma, mildly shocked. She was completely restored they saw, pink-faced and solemn as before, and quite in command of herself.

'This is when we're supposed to go down the mountain,' said Peter.

Michael crossed the few feet of earth to the tiny spring and crouched beside it. 'Could it really do any harm?' he said.

'If you're told not to drink things, you don't,' said Emma primly.

'Come on,' said Michael. 'It's only water.'

'You'll be offering me an apple next,' said Emma, and she set off across the small plateau, the way they had come.

Michael laughed and abandoned the spring. 'In that case,' he said, 'there's no point in looking for the stream that feeds the reservoir. Which is a relief because I left the map in the rucksack.'

Michael was more himself, too, Peter thought, watching him. The fear had gone, the sudden and embarrassing deference had gone. He was preparing to go home, not out of panic but because it was time. Peter wondered if he was different himself, but couldn't decide. All he knew was that he felt very faintly uneasy, as if something was unfinished. This seemed odd because the other two looked placid, satisfied.

'It's still dark,' he said, following them.

'Yes, but everything's obviously back to normal now,' said Michael, 'so that must mean that all this took the whole day to happen. It's night, but now it's the night of the day when we set out. The only problem is that the Myers must be up the wall with worry.' He slid his way confidently down over the rocks towards the place where the knapsack waited.

Peter followed, wondering if Mrs White might at that moment be holding the stone and picking up their movements in the chilly darkness.

'How long is it going to take us to get back?' he said, looking down at the village lights and trying to suppress an irrational fear that when they reached home it would be twenty years ago, or ten years in the future, and no one would know who they were.

'Quite a time,' said Michael, who seemed to be finding his way marvellously well, because, clear though the night was, there was no moon.

No moon!

Peter glanced up once or twice as he hurried down, trying not to get left behind. There had been no moon in the sky on whatever night the rainstorm had flung them into, although there ought to have been because last night the moon had been almost full. If there was still no moon, how could everything be back to normal? And yet the Aquarian had said to go down the mountain, so what else could they do?

They reached the rucksack, which had dried out pretty well, and Michael offered to have first go. Peter helped him on with it and they made their way back to where they had first deviated from the straight track.

And from there, where they had a clear view down the length of Arthur's Way, they could see a strange golden glow. It was like a globe of light, hundreds of yards across, and it moved slowly and steadily up the track towards them. Or, rather, it spread towards them, because as the front advanced the rest stayed where it was, so that the countryside was lit up behind, as though the sun was shining. It was just like watching mist bowling steadily down from the heights, or dusk creeping out of the hollows in the ground. Towards the front of the advancing wall of light moved a figure, made small by distance, that toiled its way steadily up the steepening path towards the three children – who stood on a shoulder of the mountain, not far below the summit, and watched its approach with amazement.

15 WHEN the ascending figure, in the aura of light of which it seemed unaware, was some way up the mountain, it became obvious that it was Mr Myer. Once they were sure of this the children started down towards him. Each time he glanced upwards they waved, but he didn't respond at all, just plodded on with great determination, pausing every now and then with visibly heaving shoulders and arms hanging down wearily. He had, they saw, lit up the entire valley behind him, right to the sea, and the rocks and the bristly grass were bathed in warm evening sunlight for yards and yards ahead of him.

They hurried down the mountain and he moved slowly up it, occasionally having a good look round but never, apparently, catching sight of them. At last, when they were about a hundred yards apart, the front edge of his aura of light touched them and he glanced up, jumped slightly and called, 'Where did you spring from?'

He didn't expect an answer, which was a good thing because all three were dumbfounded to see that it was they who had been encased in the darkness that had fallen on the mountain and which was only now dispersing. Peter looked behind him, up the mountain, and saw sunlight flood the slopes and flow upwards from the top so that the black night sky took on the greenish-blue tinge of a fine autumn evening.

Mr Myer followed Peter's gaze and said, slightly breathlessly, 'Odd. It's been as clear as that all day.'

'Why is it odd?' said Peter.

'Because there's been a fog warning on the radio. That's why I came up to see you safely down. You're quite a responsibility, you know. Dusk isn't far off and what with that *and* fog ...' He turned away and began to stump awkwardly downwards again. 'Better get moving,' he said. 'Had a nice time?'

Michael was looking faintly amused. 'Has it rained in the valley today?' he said conversationally.

'Oh no,' said Mr Myer, over his shoulder. 'It would have rained on you up here if it had – we're not really very far away, you know.'

Michael caught Peter's eye and grinned broadly. Emma looked thoughtful, as if she was trying to work out the mechanics of the whole thing. Neither of them seemed perturbed. They both looked scruffy, and as if they might have fallen in and out of a couple of mires on the way up – something which Mrs Myer would notice even if Mr Myer didn't – but that was all.

'What an extraordinary day,' Peter said to Michael, experimentally.

'Very interesting,' Michael agreed.

'Something to write home about,' said Peter, still testing.

'I don't think I would, actually,' said Michael. 'I don't think anyone would believe it. Anyway, you know how it is when anything really unusual happens – you're too surprised to take in the details and then afterwards you can't remember enough to tell it properly.'

This made Peter, who could remember every separate moment, feel lonely. He caught up with Emma who was ahead of him and immediately behind Mr Myer. 'What's the strongest impression on your mind at the moment?' he said conspiratorially – softly so that Mr Myer wouldn't hear.

'How worried Mrs Myer must be,' said Emma.

Peter slackened his pace until he was bringing up the rear. On this mountain, such a short time ago, they had been involved in something entirely outside their experience; how could it fade for them, like a dream, when to him it still had more substance than Mr Myer's dogged downhill walk with his attention on the path and nothing else. Peter glanced at his watch and saw that it had started again. 'What's the right time?' he called.

'Just after five,' said Mr Myer, without looking back. In his mind he was in the cottage already, the children safely under Mrs Myer's care and himself released from responsibility and shuffling through his catalogues.

Peter wound his watch hands on to five o'clock and then, thinking when they had stopped, he glanced behind him.

The Aquarian lights shone out over the black mountain top and darkness was rolling down towards him like a great wave. He opened his mouth to call a warning to the others, but it was upon him before he could speak; and the absolute shock of being plunged into a night to which his eyes were not accustomed made him stand quite still for several seconds, squinting up at the sky, his mouth open. Then he turned round quickly for the comfort of their presence, but the others were not there. The moonless darkness was every-where once more, only this time he was quite alone on the mountainside.

He had stopped so suddenly that his feet were badly placed and he slid a few inches on some loose shale, which brought him to himself. He moved to a flat-topped rock at the side of the path and crouched on it, surveying the possibilities and trying to think calmly over the persistent thought that revolved busily in his head: 'I knew it wasn't over, I knew the power was still flowing.'

He looked down at the village, so much nearer now than before, and with a feeling of desperation noted the un-mistakable differences. Lights blazed out from Mrs White's small and distant cottage, but the Myers' cottage had not even been built and the dark rolling country to the right of the track was uninterrupted, although there should have been quite a substantial farm there, with several outbuild-ings. He looked back up at the mountain top. 'It was never our Quest,' he thought, 'so what am I supposed to do?' Even his watch had stopped again, so that he felt totally deserted by everyone and everything.

All at once the sea was lit by mellow sunlight which swept across the village and towards him as if someone was drawing back a blind. On, up, it came, until it seemed to create Mr Myer – who had certainly not existed at all in the darkness – still on his way down and saying, 'Do keep up with me, there's good children.' On and on it spread, and Emma and Michael came into being, standing stock-still, Emma with her hand on Michael's sleeve, both gazing around them with startled faces. Then it reached Peter and they saw him and scrambled back to him, and he glanced behind him in time to see night peeled back, and up, and away.

'You disappeared,' said Emma. 'What happened?'

'*You* disappeared,' said Peter unhappily. 'Let's get a move on, he hasn't noticed yet.'

'What happened?' persisted Emma, walking beside him so far as the path would allow, with a kind of motherly concern. 'I turned round to say something to you and you just weren't there any more.'

'It's all right – it was only a fluke,' said Peter. 'I'll tell you about it when we get back.' His legs were beginning to ache with tiredness and his head to ache with hunger. He wanted to be as free of it all as they so obviously were, and he wouldn't talk but walked as fast as he could, knowing that they wouldn't question him if he caught up with Mr Myer.

It didn't happen again until they were past the standing stone – although at the stone itself his spine crawled and when he put out his hand, unable to resist touching it in passing, he felt something very like an electric shock in his fingers. This second time, the darkness held him for only about thirty seconds and he simply waited for it to pass, looking down at his feet, afraid to acknowledge the village of years ago. When the darkness cleared he was standing exactly where he had been, and Emma and Michael were staring at him, pop-eyed.

'Do you think if we all held hands . . .' said Emma.

'Let's just get back down,' said Peter, shrugging away her offer. He felt almost angry, with both of them, although it wasn't their fault that they weren't in it any longer. But it seemed almost like a betrayal, and in his anxiety he let his mind fill with resentment, and he accused them silently of being unsympathetic and insensitive. Somehow the concern on their faces only irritated him more, because he knew he was being unfair to them and there was absolutely nothing they could do.

When they reached the lane they walked straight past Mrs White's house, almost without thought. All they wanted to do was get back, and change, and sit down, and have something to eat. And for once Mrs Myer found herself absolutely on their wavelength, as she produced an enormous high-tea and organized a rota for the bath.

The promised fog was beginning to appear, like strands of cotton among the trees, and it was very pleasant to sit indoors, eating, and saying airily, 'But we're no later than we expected to be. And it would have been all right. There's no danger up there.'

'You realize, I suppose,' said a well-fed, sleek and tidy Michael, as they walked down the lane an hour or so later, 'that seeing Mrs White is going to be very embarrassing? We've practically got to teach our grandmother to suck eggs.'

'We could just give back the glasses and thank her for having us, couldn't we?' said Emma. 'I don't want to get involved in anything again. It might not always end happily.'

'No, no,' said Peter. 'Sorry, but we've got to tell it like it was.' He was feeling infinitely brighter and more optimistic now, and was inclined to think that his fears, and his anxieties about the thing not having finished, stemmed from the sort of depression that goes with hunger. 'She won't mind.'

And she didn't. Her lectures to Michael about keeping an open mind had been sincere. She listened carefully and Peter thought, 'That's why she's wise – because she will listen to people who know more than she does, whoever they are.'

'I'm so very grateful to you all,' she said, when the story was told. 'And I'm sorry if you were upset by any of it. I didn't *make* you go, did I? You did *want* to go?'

'Yes, of course we wanted to go,' said Emma. Mrs White's manner had been as reassuring as always and Emma no longer felt there was a danger of being involved in anything else. 'And Peter will stop disappearing now, won't he?' she went on, as if to wind up the proceedings.

Mrs White didn't answer her, and if Emma didn't notice, Peter did.

'It was quite embarrassing,' said Michael, laughing slightly. 'I don't know what we'd have said to old Myer if he'd noticed.'

When they left, the other two went out of the door first and Peter and Mrs White were left facing each other for a few seconds.

She smiled at him, her old, wise face a little sad. 'As you have seen, I don't know everything,' she said.

'It's all right,' said Peter uncomfortably.

'I don't know what happens now,' said Mrs White.

'Is it up to me?' said Peter.

'I would help you if I could,' said Mrs White, 'and I hope you believe that.'

'Yes, I believe it,' said Peter, and he caught up with the others on the long cottage path and hoped that the sense of expectancy that seemed to be in the air was really in his own imagination.

They were halfway down the lane when it happened, and this time he knew in advance that the darkness was coming because he recognized the feeling of almost electrical tension which came before it. They were in fact almost level with the Myers' cottage, which meant that Peter suffered a horrible sensation of loss, because not only did Emma and Michael disappear, the cottage vanished also.

He continued to walk the way he had been walking, with some idiotic idea that if he went on as if nothing had happened, then nothing *had* happened.

As his eyes grew accustomed to the dark, Peter realized he was at the corner of the lane, and interest made him forget fear because he saw, through the clear, starlit night, that the bend in the straight track was only just in the process of being made, and he saw the reason for it. Someone had decided to turn the original footpath into a cart track, and this track was complete up to where Peter stood. At that point, however, the straight path (which was still a public right-of-way, though barely discernible, in his own time) cut across rich ploughed fields to the village, and common sense had obviously decided that it would be foolish to lay gravel over such good farming land. Especially when there was a wide strip of poor-quality thin soil over to the right, where a ridge of the mountain, like the root of some huge tree, ran down to the coast. And so they had turned the cart track and were clearing a way for it to wind down to the village by the route that the present-day lane followed.

While Peter looked at all this, he was conscious of a sound from the direction of the village and all at once his mind made sense of what he heard. Someone was running, and now he could dimly see the figure as well as hear it, stumbling up the straight track from the village. Far behind him more people were running, and a dog seemed to have joined in because high yelping barks cut through the still air.

Sudden fierce panic hit Peter at the approach of these totally alien people who, by his own time, had been dead for perhaps hundreds of years. He dived behind the great pile of rubble and rock and weeds that had been cleared from the corner and dumped on the opposite side of the lane to the field gate. Glancing behind to see that there was no light to silhouette him, he raised his head carefully and peered out through a fringe of weeds. The fugitive was now very near to the field gate, and his gasping, wheezing breath could be heard clearly. The pursuers, in full cry and with a second excited dog to keep them company, seemed to have lessened the gap somewhat, although they were too far away to be seen clearly.

Choking with the effort, the pursued climbed the field gate and stood for a moment, shoulders heaving, staring around him desperately, obviously in no state to run any farther. He was a big man, Peter saw, wearing a tattered sort of smock and leggings, and he was either half out of his mind with fear or else half-witted. For one awful moment he turned his big, stricken face on to Peter, and Peter stared back, motionless behind his weeds, knowing that any sudden movement to duck out of sight would give him away. But the man's eyes were glazed with fear and all he seemed to see was the big mound of debris and the protection it might offer. He crawled behind it, separated from Peter only by a pile of roots and weeds, and crouched down low, his face in his hands, gasping as if he would never get his breath again.

In what seemed like seconds the pursuers reached the field gate, and they were not ruffians, as Peter had thought they might be, but simple villagers with self-righteous expressions. They spoke such a strong country dialect that he could barely make out what they said; but he heard something about 'murderer', and one of them seemed to be putting up some half-hearted defence for the fugitive, saying that he was an idiot, a looney, not responsible for his actions. The dogs flushed the man out in no time, and so enjoyed the game, as their masters dragged him, gibbering and trying to hide his big face in his hands, from his hiding place, that they never saw Peter at all.

They held the man captive and they reminded him of what he had done, which he seemed to understand – though the strange dialect made it almost unintelligible to Peter, tense with the terrible fear of discovery. It was something about a girl, perhaps the daughter of one of the men present, and they said he had killed her, and that was as much as Peter understood.

He started to say 'No, no' before Peter realized what they were going to do to him. Then he saw the rope in the hand of the leader and noticed that someone else was pointing overhead to the strong bough of an elm tree, and he plugged his ears with his fingers and buried his face in the rubble and nettles in front of him. He stayed that way for what seemed like an hour.

When fierce cramps all over his body forced him to move, he withdrew his face from the mound, spat out earth and twigs as silently as he could, and raised his head to look.

The place was empty except for the big, still figure that hung loosely from the branch, and in that instant Peter understood, and with understanding disgust and fear went. Whenever he had slipped back to in time, the power was flowing then, too. And though this power might only flow down the straight track periodically, still it was a life-force, which meant that it operated through all living things. So that when the ancient track was turned and all life, all mobile life, was sent a different way, a whirlpool was created. And in this newly created whirlpool was caught the terrible emotion of the lynching. And Peter knew exactly how to clear it, how to clean it, and he was not afraid any more.

Then the night of the past lifted, in exactly the same way as it had each time before, except that this time Peter was back in dusk and not sunlight. He got up, at the familiar, present-day corner of the lane, and he felt calm. Now it *was* over. The Dragon Power was spent, it was not flowing any longer and he didn't know when it would flow again – perhaps not even until the next autumn.

First, he decided, he would go into the Myers' cottage, and reassure the other two that he had stopped disappearing. Then he would go and see Mrs White, because as far as he knew he wouldn't be around when the power flowed again. So he would tell her what he knew, and, somehow or other, she would have to organize what was necessary to clean the unhappy debris out of the whirlpool. He was certain she would agree – unless this was his Quest and not for her to undertake.

He walked back along the lane in the misty dusk, and he pictured how it would have to be: a great procession from the standing stone to the sea along the old straight track. A procession of life to carry the force along its proper way and to sweep it past the corner that had perverted its power. A procession of as much life as possible – people, children, dogs; a carnival; the children carrying flowers and branches and everyone singing; like all the traditional country festivals there had ever been –

And if it *was* his responsibility, then he would just have to come back, somehow, at the right time –

ARTHUR'S WAY

There really are ancient tracks, like Arthur's Way, all over Britain. If you would like to know more about them and about how to discover if there is such a track in your area, you will find information in *The Old Straight Track* by Alfred Watkins and *The View Over Atlantis* by John Michell, both published by Garnstone Press, London.